LAURA ESPINAL CORPENO

7 Moons Hotel

The Amulet's Game

First published by Wise Quill LLC 2024

This novel is entirely a work of fiction. The names, characters and incidents portrayed in it are the work of the author's imagination. Any resemblance to actual persons, living or dead, events or localities is entirely coincidental.

First edition

ISBN (paperback): 979-8-9915356-0-1
ISBN (hardcover): 979-8-9915356-1-8

Cover art by Holly Dunn

This book was professionally typeset on Reedsy.
Find out more at reedsy.com

To those jumping between fictional worlds, I hope you enjoy your stay at 7 Moons Hotel.

Contents

1

A Shadowed Truth?

It was often overlooked how similar delinquents were to detectives. In essence, they were two flowering branches of the same towering tree. Similar in nature, yet different in development. But as I rode in the back of Head Detective Cromwell's car, I realized there was something else to note. Something so obvious it was puzzling. I, Avira Savio, was the flowering branch in between. The odd branch that received the perfect amount of light, but became invisible in the night's shadow. The gray line blended both sides.

The case was solved, yet I still found myself in handcuffs. My face was stuck in a tight scowl since I was forced into the old car. The smooth leather seats were peeled and rigid in the wrong places. An abrasively sweet smell assaulted my nose. An oddly cheerful jingle was muted by the thick divider. I couldn't see Cromwell but he could very well see me. My glare could have melted the tinted windows as I fixed my attention on Downtown's numerous square buildings. The car ride from a black market was tediously long with the wrong company. I couldn't enjoy the view, my thoughts were too loud and too inconclusive.

To understand my conundrum, there are a few things one must know. Boredom is the perfect fuel for... thoughtful shenanigans. Helping the greater good was a daunting task, so naturally, my attention was grabbed by the minor gripes of the people.

The small town of Verita offered entertainment to those who knew where to look. Or rather, where to eavesdrop. In the slow afternoons of Verita's town center, chatter tended to be aloft. Mundane conversations were often peppered with juicy details. Some details were enticing enough to pique my interest and prompt my hand to investigate. What harm came from that? Unsurprisingly, harm did not trail my actions.

In a short 3 weeks, I became the town's problem solver. Gallantly dubbed the "Anonymous Helper". But this gallant Anonymous Helper was growing bored of the lackluster cases. Missing heirloom? Found in a random shoe. Lost page of an irreplaceable spell book? Caught in the vents. For whatever problem, no matter how minor, I had a solution. I was quite the saving grace of the slightly frustrated folk. Especially since such issues were never taken to detective agencies. Those problems were far too minor to develop a written case for.

Most situations required me to commit the *minor* crime of breaking and entering. However, nobody cared as long as it aided them. Things were found, not stolen. My unorthodox methods gave the solutions people needed. Yet, with boredom staining my motivation, I found myself craving something else. Something *more*. A challenge that would fuel my senses and sharpen my wits.

The Case of Armeli's Chalice.

The case I solved and was ultimately being punished for.

I was barely given three hours to savor the sweet taste of victory. Frustration simmered under the cooling sensation of triumph. I despised the way the cuffs bit into my skin with every jolt of the car. Cromwell drove annoyingly slow and didn't attempt to dodge the various potholes littering the street. The thick silence between us made my mind retrace the series of events. I needed to collect my thoughts if I were to be properly interrogated.

Perhaps I committed a few "mistakes" along the way. Well, not mistakes to the authority. In essence, they were "crimes" I would never willingly list.

For once, I didn't hesitate to grab the opportunity by the throat. The Case of Armeli's Chalice wasn't public information. Challenges of that caliber weren't acquired by word of mouth. Such things required a delicate plan and a thoughtful approach. Or at least, in most cases. Cromwell's security was terribly unequipped for a quiet vampire with a purpose. Every piece of information was behind a door with a pickable lock. Even with gloves, I didn't need to touch a single thing. Cromwell had a board connecting every thread of the case.

His lines of reasoning made logical sense. But logic was multifaceted. What made sense to a detective made different sense to a criminal. All I did was stare at it long enough to find something Cromwell evidently overlooked. Well, simply put, he underestimated the desire for wealth.

Within three days, I solved the case. Yet, much like any other land, getting bested by a 21-year-old with no training was simply unacceptable. That, and the list of crimes I committed had expanded beyond breaking and entering. Of course, I knew that and so did the Head Detective.

Three hours had passed since I found Armeli's Chalice in

Armeli's Black Market auction. The old woman had placed a duplicate for Cromwell to find. If not found, a hefty sum would have been awarded to her from an insurance claim. I thought the entire case was obvious. *Too* obvious. If I had a priceless item and needed a fortune, I would have done the same.

The notion was no longer as thrilling as it once was. That instinct of obvious deceit was what criminalized me. It was more annoying than the tight monsturion handcuffs on my wrists. Strikingly bright, anyone would notice a running fugitive. Even with my vampiric strength, I wouldn't be able to break out of them.

My first time in proper handcuffs... Now what?

How was I supposed to explain myself to my mother? I had told her earlier I was visiting Neri for a girl's day out. Technically, it wasn't an entire lie. I did, in fact, visit Neri, however, the purpose of the visit was more transactional. I needed a disguise and a car. Both of which I now owed her. But that wasn't a problem. Money was never a problem for the Savio family. Finding who accepted bribes was shockingly harder. And with my recent luck and family ties, buying myself out of jail wasn't an option. I doubted Cromwell would propose a bail that didn't threaten to drain the family fortune. If it was money he wanted, he would have made that known a long time ago.

I leaned forward, close enough to fog up the divider's tinted glass. Aside from the muffled tune, Cromwell's deep voice seeped through. Unfortunately, I couldn't discern a single phrase or word from his muted conversation. Yet the tone still managed to radiate. It was a low grumble, etched with the exhaustion only several years of stressful work could bring.

Cromwell's expression flashed across my memory. Strangely, he didn't utter a single word when he arrested me. Instead, he gave me an indecipherable look. His dark eyes had a bitter twinge circulating. His thoughts nearly bled into his gaze. The look was… jarring. So much so that I stupidly allowed him to activate the cuff's stingers.

For a moment, I didn't understand my reaction. My run-ins with Cromwell were nearly routine. He made it evidently clear he wasn't fond of my title as "Anonymous Helper." Mostly by sending heavily inked letters or stopping by Savio Manor simply to scream into the lobby. (On the screaming days, I figured he was bored.)

His silence irked me more than it should have. It didn't help that his grumbling voice taunted me with indecipherable information. For once, I wasn't sure what to expect next. Would a regular procedure await me? Fingerprints, a lot of paperwork, and mug shots? The mug shot I wasn't looking forward to. I looked more deranged than stylish in my disguise. Before I could finish contemplating the Head Detective's options, the wheels crunched to a stop on the damp cement.

An electric twinge of dread swirled with my brewing antici-pation. The imposing brick building cast an angular shadow across the town square. Few people walked the sidewalk. Most stopped short and crossed the street at our two-car arrival. A bitter taste raided my tongue as Cromwell's three young towering guards lined up beside the car. Duck, Goose, and Swan awaited Cromwell's further instructions.

I, for one, was in no rush to enter the Aior Building. At least within the car, I would be able to think more sensibly. In my case, I didn't have an excuse or a proper reasoning behind my actions. Cromwell's reaction and action seemed entirely unnecessary to me. Was he just a bitter old man? Did it really bother him that I solved the case *for* him? My intentions weren't ill-mannered. Any tips were good tips if it meant solving a case and that's exactly what I did.

Goose's gruff face appeared close to the window. His orange eyes narrowed at me before opening the door.

"Alright, get out," he said as he opened the door. "Do not say a word if you know what's good for you."

Duck and Swan stood in front of Cromwell as I struggled to get out. The crisp breeze brought a cinnamon aroma to my nose. My attention centered on Cromwell as my feet met the cracked pavement. His mustache face was in a deep scowl, extenuating the deep grooves on his face. Unlike his guards, he didn't try to evade my gaze. It almost seemed like he tried to piece what stormed my mind. In reality, nothing did. The bitterness became intrigue. What was the Head Detective's next move? Was I to officially obtain the title of "delinquent"? Or was I about to receive a proper "thank you"? The second option was more far-fetched than me losing my fangs.

Aior Building's dim lighting barely illuminated the shadowed door. With the thick storm clouds looming, it almost seemed like night fell prematurely. As Cromwell stalked toward the door, his guards fanned behind me and urged me forward. They knew better than to attempt to grab my arms. My steps were more silent compared to Cromwell's brutes.

My wrists ached with every step I took. Perhaps handcuffs were an outcome I should have anticipated. However, I still didn't find them necessary. I was no fugitive. Perhaps that's what Cromwell wanted. For me to further reinforce the fact I was more of a delinquent than a detective. As if my list of crimes wasn't long enough as it was.

The door's shrill screech allowed the reality of the situation to settle in. It was naive of me to think he would turn around and shoo me away. The inside of the building was colder than the town. The air was bare of any comforting scent. The cool-toned lights flickered as he guided me deeper into the long bare hall. Cromwell's staff was scattered within the 4 story building, which was good for me. The fewer people I crossed paths with the better.

It didn't take long for me to find myself in a cramped office. Duck and Goose stood beside the arched door. Swan stood in front of me as Cromwell entered. His bushy brows raised with a smug smile.

"You better not try anything, Savio," Swan sneered. "You'll just add more time to your sentence."

He moved away from the door and ushered me in. Cromwell took a seat before me as the door shut. I remained standing, mostly because standing was more comfortable. The narrow seats could have acted like a subtle torture device. Anyone who sat would spill secrets just to leave the seat. Even if Cromwell's office wasn't an interrogation room, it felt like I had entered one. The dull walls were bare of decorations and shelves. The few windows were covered by a murky brown curtain. His large birch desk was covered by a frenzy of files and loose sheets of blank paper. A cup of coffee was forgotten by the window sill. Among the chaos of papers was a phone and a folded note.

"Take a seat," Cromwell said dryly.

I blinked at him. I was told not to talk, so I didn't respond.

"You can speak," Cromwell added exasperatedly. "You will need to speak to me if you want a good outcome."

"I prefer to stand," I replied. "Those seats are not meant for those with handcuffs."

"Fine, remain standing. The situation you created is less than comfortable anyway."

I held back my initial response. It wasn't a situation *I* created. It was a situation I *handled.* There was a difference. A very, very important difference that lacked nuance or complexity. However, I was never one to beat around the bush. I wasn't planning on granting him silence. Silence, although uncomfortable, was bearable. But a conversation? A conversation was worse.

"What's your plan Head Detective?" I asked as levelly as I could. "You didn't bring me to the processing room. Should I hope you're planning on letting me go soon?"

"You should be grateful." Cromwell's scowl shifted to annoyance. "I warned you. I told you to stay out of it and what did you decide to do?"

"Solve the case," I said matter-of-factly. "Would you have preferred if Armeli got away with it? A black market ring was taken down *and* several arrests were made."

"That is beside the point Avira," he said sharply. "You are going down a path you do not understand and I will no longer simply allow you to do it."

"What am I not understanding?" I asked sheepishly.

"You do understand your father is a very important man of business? The entire Savio family is. Having headlines of his daughter getting arrested would be an embarrassment to him."

"If he's so embarrassed, he can just drop the Savio name and use his surname again," I scoffed.

How dare he? My father was a busy man, but he wasn't a prick. I would get a cold shoulder, but he wouldn't call me an embarrassment. Anger bubbled in my chest. I took a small step forward. I didn't realize I was lingering by the door. To him, it must have looked like I was trying to make a run for it. And subconsciously, perhaps I was. I had unknowingly entered a land mine. Each word had to be carefully placed. Each action had to be precise. It was difficult to deduce what Cromwell truly had in mind. What if he was awaiting a major screw-up on my behalf? A confession of some sort?

As long as the conversation stayed between us, I didn't see anything to worry about. I'd iron out the wrinkles. He was too much of my father's friend to give the newspaper news of my arrest. I'd profusely apologize and swear I would never try anything similar ever again. I would even willingly sign an agreement. Anything that would ease his mind and not cloud my liberties. Or become a public embarrassment to the Savio Family.

Without waiting for my response, he reached for the red button on the phone.

"Bring Mrs. Savio to my office, please," he said, his eyes unwavering. "There are matters we must discuss."

2

An Unruly Punishment?

In a mere two sentences, my stomach plunged deeper than another feral fanged creature. Out of all of Cromwell's interventions, he rarely spoke to my mother about it. The notion alone was so out of pocket I thought my ears deceived me. Anger quickly shifted to a crawling dread. I was wearing handcuffs… I didn't want her to see me like that! I didn't care about Cromwell. I cared for my mother and her opinion. Of course, she knew of my… shenanigans. She never retaliated. Rather, she didn't say anything. She would give me a long look and a sigh. I tended to interpret it the way I wanted to. As I did with most things.

The panic on my face prompted Cromwell to speak again. "I told you before. The moment I felt the need to set things in order, I would. You tried your luck one too many times, Avira."

"T—This is your idea of an intervention?" I exclaimed. "I'd appreciate it more if I wasn't handcuffed."

"You don't want Reyna to see you in handcuffs? It's to be expected if you find yourself in my office," Cromwell said bluntly. "Perhaps you should take a seat. The handcuffs will be less visible that way."

My face scrunched as if I bit into a lemon. The slight smile on the Elvin old man's face made a splinter of rage blossom. There were many ways to deal with a delinquent. But I was no delinquent. Perhaps one could argue that I was no detective. Yet, involving my mother was the icing on the cake of doom Cromwell presented me with.

I could hear the clack of heels against the dull tiles get closer. Like a startled fool, I flung myself onto the torturous seat. The handcuffs dug into my skin as I forced myself to sit straight. A pained smile tugged at the corner of my lips. If looks could kill, I would have destroyed Cromwell with a single glance. My mother's gentle knock on the door made my stomach sink.

"Come in, Mrs. Savio," Cromwell called.

The door was oddly quiet as my mother swung it open. I couldn't fully turn to her as the door's wind ruffled my dark hair. Not because I was a coward, but because the damn chair made it impossible to do without wincing.

"Head Detective Cromwell, lovely day isn't it?" my mother said casually.

"I must agree with you, given the circumstances." Cromwell gestured at me. "Please, take a seat."

"Thank you, but I prefer to stand."

My mother made her way to my side and placed a hand on my shoulder. Her touch alone made me nearly burst out in an over-the-top apology. However, I wasn't going to allow Cromwell the satisfaction. I would never allow it. The look on her face made it clear that my assumption was correct. It *was* an intervention.

"Avira," my mother said gently. "I don't think I can save you from this one."

The ground could have cracked and swallowed me whole and I would have preferred it. Her cryptic delivery made taking down an organized crime ring the worst possible thing I could have done with my morning. I wanted to reach out and grab her hand, but I couldn't. My pained smile went beyond the stinging of the cuffs.

"Alright, let's not waste any more of our precious time. Your daughter has committed various crimes in the last 72 hours," Cromwell began as he stood up. "Breaking and entering, tampering with evidence, impersonating an officer, driving an unregistered car, having forged documentation, and the list goes on."

I could feel my mother's gaze on me. I tried my best not to scowl at Cromwell's pretty list of crimes. Unfortunately, all were irrefutable. I was almost thankful he didn't mention the black market in detail. Almost.

"Do you have anything to say for yourself?" Cromwell prompted with a smug smile.

"I don't see the harm in that," I said evenly. "Anyone would be commemorated for uncovering a ruse of that caliber."

"That's the problem Avira," my mother finally spoke. "You *don't* see the harm. I fear you will only take this victory as another reason to continue. That's not something I can continue to allow."

I might as well have been sucker punched. Yet, as I met her gaze, I saw past her words. There was a far reassurance.

"I... I just wanted to help," I said slowly.

"I did not ask for your help, Avira," Cromwell replied icily. "What you did cannot go unpunished. You must understand that. I will give you two options. One is a definitive and one is *if* he agrees."

My mother took out a tiny slip of paper from her purse. Discreetly, she slipped it across the smooth desk.

"Well, what is it?" I prompted.

"Jail or… Or you work at your Uncle's hotel the entire winter," Cromwell said.

I blinked at him. The second option was stranger than jail. I had worked for Uncle Julian during the summer since I was a child. A summer requirement. An unspoken rule. But for the entire winter? I could hardly believe he would agree to such a thing. Uncle Julian's rush time was governed by him and only him. Surely, he wouldn't want his problematic niece to mess up his business?

Oh, so you're trying to land me on a one-way ticket to jail? That's what I get for helping?

My mother caught my gaze and gave me a small wink. She took the phone and placed it on speaker. The silence was interrupted by the phone's droning tone. What would happen to me if he didn't pick up? Cromwell's cryptic delivery made a loop of tension tighten around my shoulders. The old detective was creative when it came to punishments. Especially for certain individuals avoiding a proper trial. It was one of the reasons why he managed to establish his own agency.

"7 Moons Hotel, Hotel Manager Julian speaking," Uncle Julian answered.

"My dear brother, how are you? It's Reyna," my mother said cheerfully.

"What do you want?" Julian replied dryly. His forced enthusiasm quickly faded to a heavy tiredness.

"It's a job offer," Reyna said. "How does a vacation sound, brother? Avira is volunteering to take over your position of Hotel Manager for the entire winter. No pay. She just wants to do something for the time being."

The line went silent for a moment. If it wasn't for the typing, I would have thought he hung up.

"Is this a prank?" he asked.

"No, this time, no," Reyna said. "So, is that a—"

"YES! Immediately yes!" Julian's voice boomed. "When does she start?"

"Tomorrow is the solstice so… tomorrow?"

"GREAT!" Uncle Julian shouted. "THANK YOU! THANK YOU SO MUCH!"

The sheer relief in his voice made me fear it was a worse punishment than jail. Yet, I knew when it was wise to openly question something and when it was not. My uncle had provided my salvation. Or at least, to the extent I could see.

I didn't know what to say. Cromwell looked as enraged as he did when he walked in. The cuffs subtly unlocked and fell onto the seat.

"You got lucky this time Avira, but I have hope this will whip you into shape," Cromwell grumbled. "I really have hope and for that, I am an idiot."

The weight on my shoulders pulled away slightly. But with the relief in Uncle Julian's voice, there was one thing I knew for sure. The punishment would be… unruly.

3

A Different Approach?

The ride from Aior Building was mostly silent. It seemed like neither of us knew what to say or how to start the conversation. In reality, it was I who should have started talking. I imagined my mother wanted some sort of explanation. Something that didn't come from Cromwell's mouth. He must have had a plethora of things to say about me. I wouldn't be shocked if he outright called me an nonredeemable delinquent. Although the arrest wouldn't go on my record, the entire ordeal made me one. But what was I to say to her?

My train of thought unfortunately pointed to a similar destination. Was I supposed to say, "Sorry Mom, boredom made me infiltrate a Black Market?" I couldn't possibly phrase it like that. I had to say something else. It was because of her I didn't find myself in the processing room. The least I could do was talk.

I took in a deep breath. The minty smell of the family car managed to pull the palpable tension away from the air. Mauricio, our chauffeur, had closed the window between us. The dense silence made me reevaluate my opinion of how bearable silence actually was. I couldn't discern what went through her mind as she stared out the black-tinted window.

From her stony expression, there wasn't much I could piece. Perhaps she too felt Cromwell's actions were... extreme? Wrong? Or at least, partially? I knew that our thoughts diverged at some point. If she shared my sentiments, she would have allowed me to find a loophole to pursue a career as a detective. However, that was the one thing a Savio could never do. It was written and sworn on by every generation. Yet, as it was in many cases, forbidden things were often the worst temptation. And even worse, I had a knack for it.

A frown furrowed my brows. With only the sound of the road filling the void, I figured if I didn't speak, I truly was a coward. Gathering all of my courage, I spoke the only thing I truly meant.

"I'm sorry," I said softly. "And um, thank you for saving me back there."

My mother tore her gaze away from the window and gave me a soft smile. Much as I wanted to do in Cromwell's office, she reached out and squeezed my hand.

"I wouldn't let Cromwell choose all the punishments. I made him believe Julian wouldn't agree," she said, her face scrunching as if an odd odor infiltrated the cabin. "It wasn't easy, but I managed to convince Cromwell my way was better."

Although her words were lightly delivered, there was the slightest edge to them. Almost like velvet and sandpaper meshing together. Perhaps just one measly apology wasn't enough. But unfortunately, in certain situations, I tended to lose my way with words. Those two pitiful sentences were all I managed to muster.

My mind was pulled back to the thrilling moment in Armeli's

Black Market. It was hidden under a basic-looking coffee shop. Shockingly, it was the coffee shop Cromwell frequented. To anyone without context, the notion was easily deemed suspicious behavior. But, after going myself, the veil between normalcy and criminal organizations was very thick.

The thrill I felt when I arrived at the auction was... electrifying. The pieces fell together before my eyes. The carefully orchestrated scheme crumbled instantly at my arrival. In my 21 years of life, there were very few triumphs that made me feel so... in my element. One shouldn't apologize for experiencing such a rare sensation. Yet, guilt swirled within the now ghostly feeling of triumph. I truly did mean my simple apology.

"I'm sorry," I said again, this time louder. "I just... I don't know what to say. Are you... mad at me?"

I felt like such a child asking that question. But I needed to know. The thought of her having a silent gripe with me the entire winter was nearly terrifying. For the first time, I feared I crossed the line. We had similar conversations in the past regarding my shenanigans. My wayward sense of adventure often led me to... interesting things. Especially in my boarding school years. However, it never involved crimes. Well, most of the time.

"No, I'm more... impressed and partially annoyed," my mother said carefully. "It's a grand achievement to you, but I don't think you realize the dangers you put yourself in."

"I do," I replied quickly.

"You don't," she said firmly. "We all may live in harmony, humans, and monsters, but that doesn't mean everyone agrees with it. It's best you don't underestimate how easy it is to get staked."

The last sentence brought an icy sliver of tension between

my shoulder blades. The once comfortable temperature in the cabin dropped to a breath-defining cold. Although frightening, it was true. Vampires had many gifts, but an old, perfectly placed stake was an ancient weakness. Along with other things, but that's a tale for another time. A black market wasn't necessarily a safe place for a meddling vampire. Or for anyone for that matter. Was I aware of all of the dangers? Admittedly, I didn't give it much thought. I had tunnel vision in Armeli's Black Market. Most people did. Everyone was too busy with their transactions to notice me. But what if they *had* noticed me? What if I had not been discreet enough? My journey of valor would have ended… badly.

I didn't realize I plunged the cabin into a stiff silence again. I didn't even notice my mother's intent stare. She was awaiting an answer.

"Right, you're right," I muttered.

"Oh, Avira," her tone softened. "You have an incredible sensing ability, but that wouldn't help you in a proper fight."

I nearly grimaced. Like I needed to be reminded of my lack of abilities. Even if I wanted to deny it, she had a point. Sensing those around me wouldn't help if I were to get attacked.

"I guess my approach could have been different," I grumbled.

"You could have just sent a note to Cromwell," my mother suggested. "Or you know, you could have not broken into his office to begin with?"

"Yeah…" I trailed off, looking away.

She squeezed my hand again, prompting me to meet her gaze. "I know you're good at this type of work, but you must remember, Avira. This isn't a job you can take. We have sworn by it."

My frown deepened. There it was again. The Savio Family

swore off that career, but it seemed like my predecessors had also sworn off giving the reason behind the radical decision. At some point, I began to wonder if my mother even *knew* the reason. Asking was futile. It had been futile for as long as I had a consciousness. I assumed it was a tragic backstory of some sort. Something straight out of a tear-jerking, sucker punching, TV novela. A drama that spanned centuries. Perhaps if I knew, I wouldn't have been so intrigued by it. But, as it was often quoted, "Ignorance is bliss".

"I know," I said finally. "I'll find something else."

It sounded far-fetched, but I was being sincere.

"I think this winter at Uncle Julian's hotel will do you some good. You have many talents, maybe another one will flourish?" my mother offered.

For once, I desperately wanted to agree. Something else had to take my interest. It simply had to.

"I'll try my hardest," I replied, confidence etched in my voice. "When spring comes, I'll have a different path."

"Don't stress yourself. You're too young to have everything figured out," she said lightly.

The car's steady pace slowed. I was so engrossed in my thoughts I didn't realize we entered Savio Estate. The manor blinked into view. The vibrant red stone glistened even in the clouded sky. Deep browns lined the gold pillars. We had already passed the majority of the towering trees. The passing breeze made the branches look as if they were dancing to a silent tune. The smooth pavement became a slightly rough cobbled road. My eyes fixed on the dazzling fountain. Much to my surprise, it wasn't running.

As the car pulled to the circle, I spotted something even more disconcerting. Francis, our longest-employed staff member, had something square towering beside him. My vision focused and the reality of the situation sunk in. Beside him was not a peculiar decoration. It was…

"Luggage?" I exclaimed, I nearly hit the top of the car. "Already?"

"The solstice is tomorrow," she reminded me as the car eased to a stop. "The 7 Moons Hotel you'll be working at is near Tionel Mountains. Not the one in Calya City, so if you don't leave now you won't get settled in in time."

I blinked in response. Francis had packed at least 8 suitcases of who-knew-what. A nervous spark ran down my spine. I knew the solstice was quickly approaching, but I was hoping I would be able to have a meal with my parents before then. Or at least walk in and relax for a bit? Although I was grateful, I wasn't necessarily eager to become a Hotel Manager.

I quickly exited the car and met my mother beside the luggage.

"And what about the helicopter? If I take that I can stay here a bit longer?" I suggested quickly.

"Your father is using it," my mother said, taking both of my hands. "I wish I would be able to keep contact with you more but I must tie up business with my tailors. And you know how tedious that is."

My bewildered expression reflected off of her yellow eyes. Cromwell made sure it felt more like a punishment rather than a working vacation. But, in truth, I wasn't going to give him the satisfaction of my brewing nerves.

"Oh, okay," I said. "I won't get into trouble, I promise you that."

My mother pulled me into a warm hug and then cupped my face. "A little bit of trouble is good for the soul. Just, don't go overboard."

I nodded slowly as she pulled her hands away. "So, I just have to manage the hotel for the winter? That sounds easy enough."

My mother let out a small sigh. "Not entirely. Cromwell accepted my suggestion only because he wanted to implement a clause."

"A clause?" I echoed. "What type of clause?"

That dirty trickster. I should have known.

"You cannot receive more than five 1-star reviews by the guests. And, at the end of the three months, you must have a favorable percentage from the staff approvals."

"Five. Five 1 star reviews in 3 months?" I asked indignantly. "He does realize that's not entirely reflective of the Hotel Manager right?"

I wasn't concerned about the staff. I was no villain. Surely, they'd like me?

She shrugged and granted a sympathetic smile. "That's what he said. But don't worry, I'm sure you'll find a way to keep that from happening. Or undo them before then. If not..."

"If not what?"

Her face scrunched. "He didn't tell me. He told me he's contemplating another option. Perhaps something similar to jail?"

My stomach dropped. The stakes were higher than I originally anticipated. I took in a deep breath, ironing out my simmering nerves. That was exactly what he wanted. He wanted me to feel like managing a hotel was the worst possible punishment. He wanted me to regret busting Armeli's Black Market. I was not going to give him that satisfaction. Although tainted, my victory was still sweet.

"Okay, whatever it is, I won't find out," I said confidently. "I will run this hotel better than Uncle Julian. I can promise you that."

"Oh, you're a Savio. I'm sure you will."

Francis loaded my luggage into the back and gave me a wisp of a smile. The old butler didn't speak often, but his silence wasn't uncomfortable. His eyes tended to speak more sincerely than most people's mouths. His gaze nearly glittered as he placed the last suitcase and opened the car door for me. As I went back into the car, he made sure to give me a double thumbs up, with a look that said, "Good luck, you're going to need it."

However, relying solely on luck was for fools. What I needed was a plan.

* * *

It would have been a lie if I confessed I slept the entire ride. My mind was far too awake for slumber. I kept my eyes closed for the majority of the journey. I found it aided my thinking, or on special days, my scheming. The situation seemed to be a blend of both. I quickly decided my approach would be simple. But for that, I needed to retrace Uncle Julian's typical routine.

In all of the summers I worked, I practically had his day-to-day memorized. Uncle Julian did everything you'd expect a Hotel Manager to do. He greeted every guest with an unwavering fanged smile. A smile that excessively displayed the sharpness of his teeth. (Why? Well, some people were really fond of fangs. It immensely helped with tips for some forsaken reason.) Besides excessively smiling, he'd manage the staff, oversee the budgeting, maintenance, paperwork, and among other details one shall be spared of. In essence, it was a glorified, overworked, certified snooze fest. In the case of a normal hotel, that's what was to be expected.

However, 7 Moons Hotel was hardly a normal hotel. It was one of the few hotels that welcomed a proper blend of Humans, Monsters, and Supernaturals. And with that came… different issues that required different solutions. Issues I never saw properly addressed. Whenever a covert situation arose, someone would whisper the details to Uncle Julian and he would simply leave. Did he ever bother to share the details? No. That vampire was so tight-lipped I couldn't even get a proper dose of gossip.

Yet with all of those factors considered, I didn't feel the familiar zap of butterflies in my gut. Yes, anticipation gripped me like a curious giant, but it didn't threaten to crush me. Instead, I classified it as more of an… unwelcome embrace. As if an impending doom had infiltrated my senses. On second thought, one could call that nervousness or I was simply being dramatic. I didn't like either of those options.

I'll just follow whatever guide Uncle Julian has for me and try not to piss anyone off. I don't think there's a plan simpler than that.

Oddly as the thought finished, my mother's voice circled back to the surface.

"A little bit of trouble is good for the soul. Just, don't go overboard."

Curiosity simmered under my circling thoughts. What could she have meant? I was about to get access to all of the knowledge Uncle Julian had. The only perk I could foresee. That certainly came with the temptation of shenanigans. However, I meant what I promised. My shenanigans were to be kept at a bare minimum. I was not in the mood to find out Cromwell's plan b nor would I ever be.

The rough jerk of the car made my eyes snap open. The

vibrant 7 Moons Hotel dawned on the dark horizon. I swallowed down my festering nerves and opened the window. The air had a different sense of tranquility. One that could only be found during a pelting rainstorm. One I had subsequently muted until I arrived. Thick cold droplets pelted the blue cobbled street. Night had fallen, but the hotel acted like a beacon in the near distance. Strong cool lights danced and marked the clouded sky with its presence. Towering statues lined the wide road. Each statue was frozen in the specific sequence of an unknown dance. I could barely look at them directly. The glittering marble acted like a road hazard.

It was the perfect introduction to the 7 Moons Hotel. The angular horseshoe building was a deep blue. Arched windows were highlighted with white and what seemed like dancing flamed lanterns. Six pillars stabbed the sky, each sporting a false moon. The 7th pillar was empty, perfectly placed to line up at midnight with the dazzlingly bright moon I couldn't see. A large, blinking neon sign buzzed loudly as we drove past it. Right behind the hotel, the Tionel Mountains was the picturesque backdrop so many guests sought for the past 2 centuries. It was a mere outline in the shadows of the night.

My eyes focused on the entrance. Much to my surprise, I spotted 5 people with umbrellas. The tallest one of the bunch was… Uncle Julian. Even at a distance, I could recognize my eccentric uncle. His attire nearly glittered as much as the hotel did. He wore dazzling orange pants and an even brighter shirt to match it. His smile was the most genuine I had ever seen. He held a small suitcase in his other hand.

I forced myself to look past the small crowd. The empty car lots made some of the tension melt away like a slow crawling wax. Melting, but still present. My hands grew clammy against the leather seats. I didn't realize my leg was bouncing more than a ball in a tight space. The moment had dawned and it was up to me to seize it. Much easier said than done. I suddenly wished I had the ability of invisibility.

The car crunched to a stop. Before I could collect my thoughts, Uncle Julian flung the door open.

"Sobrina!" Uncle Julian yanked me out of the car and pulled me into a tight embrace. "Thank you! Thank you! Thank you!"

"You're going to crush me," I strained.

"Oh, sorry Avira. I'm much too enthusiastic about this." He let go and turned to his staff. "My dearest Head Staff, this is Avira Savio, my dear niece and your new boss for the winter. Please show her the ropes and aid her in whatever she needs."

It was a nice way of saying, "Don't let her burn the hotel down, " and I really appreciated that. Uncle Julian handed me the umbrella with an unwavering smile.

I smiled the best I could and scanned the unfamiliar faces. Although they didn't share Uncle Julian's excitement, they didn't seem to hate the idea either. The older faces scrunched slightly, but I decided to blame the howling wind for that. The tall, broad man with 6 red eyes took a step forward. His smile was sincere as he extended his hand.

"Miss Savio," he said, shaking my hand. "My name is Onyx. I am the proud Head of Security of this 7 Moons Hotel."

"Pleased to meet you," I said with a smile.

The rest followed Onyx's example and lined up behind him. Right after him was a sweet-looking middle-aged woman. Her smile beamed with genuine excitement.

"Welcome Miss Savio! My name is Betsy!" She took my hand with both of hers. "I'm the Head of Events and Cleaning and well, anything you can possibly need."

"Now, now Betsy," Uncle Julian chimed in. "The last part is the role of a concierge and my niece will not have one."

Betsy smiled apologetically and stepped aside, giving way to a young man a few years older than me.

"Miss Savio, I am Griffin. Front desk and miscellaneous task runner, at your service." He bowed over my hand. His slight smile revealed the tips of his fangs. They were much smaller than mine. The way his ears rounded made me believe he was half-human.

I smiled, although, at that point, my cheeks were twitching from holding it so long. Lastly, a small woman appeared in front of me. Her mouth was more animalistic. She seemed to be a Chetra.

"Head Chef Z," she said proudly. "All of your food needs will be exceptionally met."

The staff lined up and collectively said, "Welcome to 7 Moons Hotel!"

"Thank you," I said as evenly as I could. "I'll do my best to keep things running smoothly."

The staff nodded politely. Perhaps they thought my words were empty. However, only time would allow me to prove them otherwise. Uncle Julian turned to me once again.

"I left a handbook in your room so if you have any questions, don't call me. Your evaluation starts now, but check 7 Moons Review Monitor in 4 days." His voice dipped to a whisper. "Your mother told me about the situation. Don't do anything I wouldn't do. Just keep things as they are and you'll do fine. Oh and, do *not* explore the hotel tonight. I will know."

I nodded slowly. "You leave the hotel in good hands,"

"Yes, I am," he agreed. "Now, I'm off! Have a lovely winter everyone!"

He didn't hesitate to help Francis unload my excessive luggage and plop his in. Without waiting any longer, he dove into the car and the black vehicle quickly faded into the distance. I tried to smile once again. The staff stared at me with a blend of curious and skeptical gazes. For a moment, I wished I had the ability to read minds.

Most turned away and walked into the hotel without saying another word. All except one. The human named Betsy.

"Miss Savio," Betsy said with a smile. "I'll be your right hand for the winter. Follow me, I'll call for the luggage. It'll be a long night!"

4

A New Old Building?

The night could have been eternal within the old walls of the 7 Moons Hotel. For the first time, my expectations were blurred by my swirling thoughts. Two luggage boys blinked into existence, touched the luggage, and swiftly vanished. Tension had woven a heavy cape over my shoulders. I tried to keep my emotions tucked under the facade of my smile. First impressions mattered more than most people willingly credited. Although the other staff members had retreated into the hotel, I still had Betsy. The middle-aged woman had a warmer smile. However, a smile could hide many things. Was it a polite smile? Was it forced? Or was it genuine?

It doesn't matter. As long as things go smoothly from here on out, she'll likely speak positively of me to others. If I'm a blubbering fool, that will also reach their ears.

My eyes trailed up the five-story building. A certain cold had infiltrated the humid air. The lanterns barely fought off the chill that draped the environment. My grip on the umbrella tightened subtly. Betsy didn't waste a moment and twirled toward the towering oak doors. I forced my apprehension into the deepest crevices of my being and focused. As soon as the doors swung open, my future for the next three months unfolded.

A massive domed-shaped lobby dawned before me. Uncle Julian had evidently renovated the place. A vintage luxury radiated from the moment I entered. The creme-colored walls were lined with deep burgundy. The domed ceiling was covered in various paintings and patterns. Hanging from it was the largest chandelier I had ever seen. A thick red chain held the twinkling lights. To either side of me were the wings that led to the rest of the hotel. The delicate scent of myrrh helped cut the tension in my muscles. The reception desk was proudly at the farthest end of the lobby. Two gold-encrusted elevators were off to the side. Nearly disappearing into the corner was a thin, blue door.

"Quite the sight isn't it?" Betsy prompted. "It didn't look like this last winter. Mr. Savio had a year-long renovation, which is why the hotel doesn't have any guests right now."

The lobby was big enough to house 200 people comfortably. Lounging areas spotted the marble floor. The plush seats were very inviting. Several tables of small amenities were situated between them.

"I see," I said slowly. "And does this location usually get busy?"

"Eh, it depends on your definition of busy, Miss Savio," Betsy continued. "This hotel is the oldest one of the bunch so people rarely come over here. At least compared to the city locations. We'd see a couple hundred guests and event rentals."

I wanted to believe the grand reopening would be slow as well. However, people were often very similar to moths. With all the glamour and lights, I expected a crowded lobby. The reservations I had yet to see would only confirm that.

"I've worked in the summer, but my Uncle would keep me away from here," I said as lightly as I could. "I'm sure it won't be so different."

"That's good to hear." Betsy led me toward the narrow blue door and gave me a pensive glance. "I hope you don't think the other Head Staff members aren't happy to have you here. We were just… surprised by the sudden change, that's all."

Heck, me too.

"I can assure you all it won't give anyone a hassle," I said reassuringly. "It'll be smooth sailing for the winter."

"Don't worry Miss Savio." Betsy stopped before the blue door. "We were all new here once. I can assure you nobody will give you a negative review over something small."

"Oh, so you know about…"

"About Mr. Savio's evaluation? Yes."

I withheld a sigh of relief. The last thing I needed was for the hotel staff to know about my dealings with Cromwell. I silently thanked my uncle. My eyes moved between the door and Betsy. The door was unlabeled. At first glance, it seemed like a utility closet. Would a utility closet be my room? My Uncle couldn't be that cruel… Could he? My look of confusion prompted a quick explanation.

"This is the entrance to the Head Staff Hall. All of us have an office here, including Mr. Savio," Betsy explained.

She opened the door revealing a long, dark corridor. Gentle star-shaped light fixtures hung from the tall ceiling. The warm light flickered like an open flame, casting a variety of dancing shadows. A few deep brown doors lined either side of the deep red walls. Each was labeled with the Head Staff's name in delicate handwriting. My eyes traveled to the end of the corridor. The mostly dull space was saved by a beautiful stained glass window. It proudly displayed 7 Moons Hotel. Every moon glittered under the low light.

Betsy quietly led me to the room next to the window.

"This is Mr. Savio's office," she said. "I can't open it, I'm not authorized. But you're the new Hotel Manager so Mr. Savio's office is now *your* office."

My own office. I would be lying if I said that didn't please me. That also meant I had access to all of the hotels… covered shenanigans. I wanted to believe Uncle Julian was as meticulous of a record keeper as he was a decorator. Betsy eyed the knob. She nearly lingered behind the random snapping plant. Was I supposed to do something? Did I miss a cue?

"What happens if an unauthorized person goes in?" I asked, genuinely curious.

Betsy's expression became an interesting blend of emotions. The memory nearly danced across her widening dark eyes. She patted her hand on her thick black hair as if to squash the thought away.

"Uh, well, Mr. Savio made us swear not to speak of it so… You can access all of that information in the archives if you're *really* curious."

My serious expression cracked with a peculiar smile. She took a small step back as if she regretted her word choice. I was not there to torture the lovely Betsy. My smile mostly confirmed my suspicions. 7 Moons Hotel had plenty of interesting moments. Moments that were waiting to be rediscovered by a new, curious mind.

My hand reached for the matte bronze knob. The metal zapped my skin as I pushed it open. The hinges screeched in retaliation and gave way to an office worthy of Uncle Julian. It was the epitome of light academia. White curtains draped over the stained glass windows. Statues of owls and ancient heroes were perched on stone pedestals. Unlit candles were placed in bronze holders. The ghostly scent of myrrh intensified. Upon the desk was a leather-bound book and a note that elegantly displayed my name. My feet were silent against the polished birch floors. I reached for the leather-bound book. Unsurprisingly, it was the manual Uncle Julian promised. The thick book was cool to the touch. In a pinch, it could easily be used as a self-defense weapon.

A Dummies Guide to 7 Moons Hotel (Hotel #13)

I plucked the neat note to find a typed letter.

Avira,

Do not mess this up. You're very lucky I'm exhausted and desperately need a break. Remember, this is a grand opening. I don't normally leave these important events to someone as inexperienced as yourself, but I can proudly say there is very little you can mess up. Everything for the grand event is planned to perfection. All you have to do is be there and not annoy the guests or staff. Whatever money you make me lose you will personally be responsible for.

With love,

Uncle Julian.

"Ah," I muttered. "That makes a lot more sense."

I found it far too strange he would leave the hotel to his delinquent niece without a contingency plan. Given the circumstances, blame was hardly something I could place on him.

I turned to Betsy who lingered by the door. "Should I review this here?"

"No need, you can come back any time," Betsy reassured, gesturing to the calendar behind me. "Since you're here for the winter, I thought it would be a nice idea to cross out the days as you go. You know, it's nice to see a visual countdown."

That was incredibly nice of her. I didn't expect such a sweet gesture so soon. "How about I cross the first day now?" I offered with a smile. "Or is that cheating?"

"I think that would be a great idea, Miss Savio," Betsy agreed. "We're just shy of midnight, so that doesn't count as cheating in my eyes."

I took a bold red marker and slashed the dawning solstice. The feeling was satisfying, although not entirely warranted.

"The schedule is inside," Betsy continued. "Tomorrow is a very important day so I should show you to your room. Chef Z has already prepared an excellent dinner! There are ethically sourced blood bottles *and* a blood-infused steak waiting for you!"

I quickly obliged. As soon as I closed the door behind me, Betsy's cheerful smile returned. Her slightly heeled shoes clacked on the polished marble floor. Her pace had quickened, perhaps to shake off her lingering nerves. As soon as she met the elevator, the doors opened with a happy ding.

"After you, Miss Savio," she said cheerfully. "Mr. Savio made sure to give you the best suite possible."

"Oh, that's oddly nice of him," I replied. My mind was immediately pulled back to the summers. "I would get a very messy corner of his office and a sad tray of snacks."

I stole a glance at the pearly buttons. The numbers were a bold black. Five stories, but only four available floors? How… *peculiar?* Uncle Julian was the type of man who would use every inch of space available to him. Why would he leave out the 5th floor?

Betsy pressed the top pearly button. The elevator smelled faintly of rich chocolate and strawberries. Beside the elevator's shiny buttons were a small stool and a basket of random amenities. The lush red carpet felt like a cloud under my feet. The shiny gold doors closed without a single sound. A very jazzy tune infiltrated the elevating chamber.

I glanced at Betsy as the elevator rose to our destination. She maintained the smallest smile on her face. Perhaps she was still in "customer service," mode? I wasn't a customer, but I appreciated the effort. A comfortable silence spread between us, but curiosity blossomed. Not about the 5th floor. That was a task for me alone.

The hall blinked to life as the doors opened. A velvety red carpet greeted us instantly. Various lit statues provided a warm light to the long halls. Thunder became a distant rumble. Uncle Julian made sure the exposed walls were covered by a small painting of some sort. Oddly, it didn't make the hall feel cluttered. It was a nice decorative touch. It gave the impression of a museum rather than a hotel. Multiple brown doors lined either side of the hall. At the farthest end, the hall curved into a different area. The sign was far too small for me to read.

With every step I took, there was the slightest flicker. The luminous lights nearly acted like open flames to a howling wind. A spreading cold seeped through the smallest cracks in the ceiling. Oddly, there was a swirl of heat pushing through. The contrasting temperatures were subtly unsettling. The slightest pitter-patter of our feet almost doubled as we moved closer to the other end of the hall.

"This place was *fully* renovated, right?" I asked after a moment. The magnetized warmth almost seemed to be following us.

Betsy's face scrunched slightly. "Yes? I don't know why the lights were flickering so much. This hotel has seen plenty of storms."

Plenty was an understatement. The hotel had a face lift, but was the overall structure reinforced? The mere thought of the ceiling caving in made a loop of tension spring to life. This 7 Moons was vastly different than the one in Calya City. It gave me an entirely new impression. Or perhaps it was the fact my circumstances were different.

Calya's 7 Moons was a nest of movement. Staff would run up and down the halls. Music would float down the long halls and common rooms. The staff that kept the hotel running smoothly was *visible*. I knew the hotel wasn't entirely empty. Uncle Julian likely kept the night crew finding every little imperfection till dawn. Yet, where were they? They behaved more like ghosts than ghosts themselves. And more surprisingly, where were the ghosts? Old buildings had at least *one* residential ghost.

There were so many peculiarities, my mind naturally drifted to Betsy.

"Mind if I ask you a question?" I started. "It doesn't have to do with the building."

"Anything!" Betsy responded as she guided me to the left.

"Why did you decide to work here?"

"Do you want me to be honest with you?"

"Yes please,"

Betsy took a deep breath. "It's the perks. My family looked at me like I went mad when I said I was going to work for this 7 Moons. I'm not sure why. I doubt it's because there are rarely full humans working here. I think it's because I chose the most remote location instead of the ones in the cities."

I nodded slowly. She may have blamed the location, but I had a feeling her family thought something else. Monsters,

Supernaturals, and Humans have been integrated for more than 300 years. However, even with time healing old war wounds, a select few were still wary of intermingling so… *casually*. (You know, without an ultra-wide array of weapons at all times).

"Oh I see, that makes sense," I said after a moment.

"I came here when I was 24, now I'm 45, so I basically learned how to adult here properly." Betsy chuckled at the memory. "That's how I became a double Head. And I'm still the youngest of the Head Staff!"

"I'm sure you've done a great job for Uncle Julian to keep you around so long," I said genuinely.

"Eh, if it's good enough for him and the customers are happy, then I think it's a good job." Betsy eased to a stop in front of the only black door.

She had led me away from the small sign and into the left wing of rooms. My room's door was the only one that looked down the entire hall.

Betsy reached into her pocket and gathered three items. A vintage bronze key, a pink card, and a cellphone. "Here is room 437 in Alterin Hall and your home for the winter. I really hope it's up to your liking, Miss Savio. If you need anything I placed my direct number in the handbook and on this cellphone."

I took the items from her. The 7 Moons Hotel logo glimmered on every item.

"The key is universal for the hotel, so make sure to keep it on you at all times," she instructed. "The 7 Moons issued cellphone has the direct number that all of the staff has access to. If someone needs you, they'll call you and vice versa."

"Thank you very much, Betsy," I said with a smile. "Go and rest calmly, I won't call tonight."

Relief seeped into her smile. "Thank you, Miss Savio! Rest well. We have a very busy day ahead of us."

She was right. A proper grand opening was riding on my shoulders. I needed to read the dummy guidebook before I could think of sleeping. How hard could it be? The night would give me enough time to review Uncle Julian's guide. I didn't favor sleeping so little, but if I had to, I would.

As Betsy disappeared around the corner I turned my attention to the door. The dark wood had slight grooves, giving it the feel of a seared-in pattern. I took a deep breath as I swiped the pink card. The cloak of tension had fully melted away from my shoulders. The simmering anticipation I held seemed to have subdued with the walk. Perhaps things weren't going to be too complicated. I had a handbook, and my own room, and at least I was able to comfortably converse with a staff member. It was small progress, but good progress.

With a gentle nudge, the door smoothly opened. The storm's thunderous symphony had infiltrated the room before I did. My towering luggage neatly lined the deep brown walls. A gentle smell of jasmine was aloft. Soft streams of incense made swirling patterns in the warmly lit room. As I stepped in, I fully took in the room I would call my abode for my winter trial.

Uncle Julian had certainly given me the best suite 7 Moons Hotel had to offer. It looked more like a small apartment than a hotel room. A small hall led to a lush sitting area, directly to the side was a kitchen, and deeper into the room was the massive bed. The decor was much like his office. The shimmering white curtains trembled at the storm's fury. The hardwood floor creaked under my subtle movements. A water mirror was placed off to the side. As I looked deeper, I immediately spotted it. Draped on the prettily made bed was the uniform.

Oddly, the sight didn't repulse me. I took a few ginger steps closer. A new sensation mingled with my easing nerves. My eyebrows raised in a blend of delight and genuine surprise. The uniform was… incredibly stylish and not as soul-sucking as I expected it to be. The tailored black jacket had a subtle sheen. Gold embroidery made flowers and vines across the shoulders. Placed beside it was a pearly white shirt, a tailored black pair of trousers, and a black string of fabric. At the very end were two crimson beads.

My hand hovered over the beads. I had seen something similar on Uncle Julian's uniform before. But under the warm scattered light, I noticed something else. There were the subtlest engravings. A pattern that was not just a point of fashion. It was a charm. A defensive charm against medium levels of magic.

"How interesting…" I muttered to myself.

It made total sense. Magic was a part of daily life. Some practitioners were more… sneaky in their use of magic. Most people had some sort of charm. At least to alert them. However, not to the caliber of which I now possessed. A small twinge of excitement blossomed in my chest. I wanted to believe my routine wouldn't be mundane. There was plenty of room for fun. Coordinated fun. *Hidden* fun.

I glanced at the TV mounted on the wall. Directly underneath it was a small red button. It was sealed with a see-through plastic. The lock gave the impression of a keyhole. A panic button?

"Wow, this room is really equipped with everything…" I muttered under my breath.

I walked to the tray of food on the round table. My stomach grumbled at the thought. The situation with Cromwell made me skip lunch and my designated snack time. Whatever was under that tray would be devoured without a second thought. I didn't waste any more time. I tossed my umbrella and took the handbook with me. Awaiting me was a glorious blood infused steak and mashed potatoes. The savory smell was mouthwatering.

The handbook's spine cracked as I sunk my teeth into the tender meat. The night would be long, but it would be entertaining. A small smile tugged at the corner of my lips. The first page was a warning.

#13 7 Moons Hotel.

Do not allow access to the Restricted Area. The fifth floor is off-limits to guests. Only the Hotel Manager can access it. Visit page 231 for more information.

Haha. A fun, long night indeed.

5

A Renewed Order?

There were three important things I learned from the gracious little handbook. Listed in no particular order were the following:

1) The 5th floor was the Restricted Area.

2) There was a lovely detachable map to every hidden passageway's entrance and exit, normal entrances and exits, and known locations, such as a ballroom, and other snazzy places.

3) I was incredibly screwed.

The third conclusion was an expected slap across the face. I had somehow managed to underestimate the sheer involvement of a 7 Moons Hotel Manager. So much so, that it pushed the thrill of the Restricted Area and secret passages away from my mind. How? Well, I underestimated how much of a workaholic Uncle Julian was. The details made my mind buzz like a funky radiator. Every week at 6 am, a meeting ran for 20-50 minutes to lay out the plan with the Head Staff. However, on grand openings, the meeting commenced at 5 am *and* was held in the Gudiern Theater with the entire staff.

The sheer thought sent a zapping eel down my spine. Worst of all, the information was imprudently introduced to me. *After* spending the entire night reading the handbook and taking in every detail.

It would have been nice if the schedule had been placed at the beginning rather than the very end. I would have skimmed instead of plotting my covert adventure! The crisp white paper had three purposes. My routine, a checklist for myself, and a very basic guide to leading the meeting. In essence, it was the foundation for a smooth sailing winter.

Yet after reading it, I quickly understood why Uncle Julian didn't hesitate nor question my sudden job offer. I had to memorize every guest's name and room number. It seemed that simply asking was seen as rude to him. I had a great memory, but after the first twenty, the details jumbled together. Beyond that, at the cusp of dawn, twice a week I was to evaluate every public room. Everything had to be perfectly placed and presentable. If the air was bare of any scent, I had to correct it. Heavens forbid the air smelled like… air. After that, I would have to survey the coming weeks' events and sign my approval. Finally, at 6 am, the meeting would start. Then… well, merely listing it would make exhaustion raid any mind.

I was very, very thrilled to do all of that.

With only a nap to fuel my day, maintaining a vibrant smile was an uphill battle. A 14-hour shift would feel eternal. A true punishment. It nearly made me regret my past choices. Nearly. Perhaps avoiding a Black Market would be better next time. Eh, perhaps not. The tasks ahead were making my thoughts nonsensical.

As the clock struck 5 am, the thick white curtains pulled open. A deep sigh escaped my lips as I rose from the chair.

Within 10 minutes, I had to become "Savio Manager Ready". There was an entire chapter dedicated to that. Uncle Julian's extensive routine was borderline madness. He had an incredibly meticulous process. I took the liberty of blurring it into 3 simple steps. Freshen up, put on the uniform, and smile when necessary. My teeth were pretty enough. His dental regimen included adding gold dust at the fang tips. Clearly, I wasn't in the mood for a bedazzled mouth.

As I adjusted the string under my collar, my gaze fixed on the view. The storm pulled away to reveal the sun-tinted sky. From my room, I could finally see the Tionel Mountains. The dark veil shed, giving way to sharp icy snow caps and specks of green. The breeze at 5 am had a different blend of serenity. Light and pleasant, it managed to alleviate the twisting tension. The scent of rain lingered as it blew through the open window. As oranges infiltrated the once-dark sky, the winter solstice fully settled in.

My job as a stellar Hotel Manager had officially started.

I took in a deep breath. The day would be... nice. If mistakes were to be made, they were to be minor. Was that delusional? Given the circumstances, yes, probably. Yet, I wanted to believe the day would be smooth sailing. A walk through the entire hotel was favorable. I held the handbook close to me as I centered my thoughts. Not that I needed it, but it completed the look.

My mind managed to retain most of the useful information. The little map seared onto my memory after staring at it for 10 minutes. I had my father to thank for that little perk. The fourth floor had the most guest rooms, but it also housed Alvera Library. My first destination. I was partially relieved I only had to see the grander common rooms. The smaller ones weren't my duty.

It's easy and simple. I can hardly mess this up.

I glanced at the loudly ticking clock. With taking the normal halls and minor delays, I had roughly 20 minutes. A piece of Crimson Cake. Without wasting any more time, I stepped out. As my feet met the smooth carpet, I felt a strong tug in my gut. No, it wasn't nerves catching up to me, it was something more distinct. Something more... *instinctive.*

I was no longer alone on the 4th floor.

It was hard to explain, but I could sense someone. The accumulated stress tricked my sensing abilities into thinking I was in danger. I usually had that ability turned off for obvious reasons. Having it on all the time was far too overwhelming, given the heightened caliber of my skill.

My steps were silent as I made my way down the vast hallway. The tug was leading me to my destination. Closing my eyes, I could nearly see the exact movements. A gently warm sensation flooded my senses.

A... human?

My pace quickened along with my racing thoughts. To my knowledge, the entire fourth floor was empty. It was empty when I first arrived with... Betsy. Was it Betsy? She was the only human I could think of. I sharply turned the corner. Allowing the thought to simmer was potentially dangerous. The sooner I confirmed my suspicion, the better. I couldn't afford to have intruders on the first day. Uncle Julian's security was stellar compared to Cromwell's. A blaring alarm would pierce through the moment any suspicious movement was detected.

The lights flickered as I came upon the tall oak doors. A passing breeze brought the mystifying scent of sandalwood to my nose. The door was cracked open enough for me to peer in. The human's shadow was mostly still. Their hands moved as if they were playing an invisible harp. A snake of tension slithered up my back. I crept even closer. My hand rested on the icy bronze knob. Would the door screech if I pushed it open? The gap wasn't enough for me to sneak in. Evidently, whoever played the invisible harp had no idea of my presence.

My face nearly touched the door's edge, but I finally saw who it was. Placing a fresh bouquet was the one and only… Betsy. The tension in my gut loosened. She was completely oblivious to my presence. Betsy's soft humming filled the quiet library as she placed the deep blue vase in the perfect position.

"Betsy, what are you doing here?" I asked.

"Miss Savio!" Betsy exclaimed, nearly knocking over her hard work. "I—I didn't see you come in."

I took a good look at the Head of Events. Deep circles adorned her face. A tired smile barely rose to her eyes. It almost seemed like she didn't leave for the night. Her uniform was still on. She still had her umbrella by her side. I was very grateful she didn't have a fight reflex. She could have very easily whacked me.

"You didn't go home?" I questioned.

I could run well with a nap, but humans? It was often a very bad idea to attempt. Their rationality and capacity to deal with people depleted faster with exhaustion hovering.

"I did. For… three hours," she admitted gingerly. "I just wanted to come earlier and inspect the rooms. I thought I'd do it for you since it's your first day."

My expression softened. Betsy was far too kind for her own good. That, or she didn't trust me as a Hotel Manager yet. It was understandable. Working hard for a year and then management decided to put a 21-year-old in charge? I would be very wary of me too.

"Thank you, but you really didn't have to do all that," I said gently. "If you're on the fourth floor then that means you…"

"Yes," she said proudly. "I already checked the Red Lady Lounge, Echo Ballroom, Gudiern Theater, Goldight Meeting Room, Lucrest Pool, and Pinicale Bar. This is the last one."

"Wow," I said in awe. "I guess that means I should head to my office and—"

Before I could finish my sentence Betsy grabbed a file and pen from her briefcase. "No need, I brought the list with me."

The smooth papers already had the places I had to sign marked with a bold *x*. I flipped through to see my uncle had already signed off. 7 Moons Hotel needed my approval as well? Oh, how fancy.

I traced the list of events, my gaze settling on the boldly inked letters.

"Moonlight Strike Ball happens the night before the Spring solstice," Betsy said, she nearly beamed. "And guess what? It's a masquerade ball! I've been planning it ever since Mr. Savio green-lit the renovation!"

"Oh, a masquerade ball? I've never been to one of those."

"You'll love it! But first, we have to get through the winter," Betsy reminded me.

I tried not to let the doubt seep into my smile. The winter was long…Those one stars… I pushed the thought aside, taking the papers. I didn't waste any more time and quickly signed my name. The hotel operated weekly. The grand opening had an impressive lineup I didn't quite read. I would definitely have another opportunity to ruin the surprise for myself.

"Thank you, Miss Savio," Betsy said as she took the file. "I should have one more for you to sign later on. It's for the final week of winter."

"Just bring it to me wherever I find myself," I replied.

"Well then, let's go to the meeting," Betsy advised. "Most of the staff is already there and they are very eager to meet you!"

My mind flashed to page 213: The Meeting.

It would be futile if I didn't admit how my stomach sank to my feet. I smiled at Betsy in an attempt to wave off any of her own concerns. Her expression didn't lean toward concern. Rather, her tired expression danced with intrigue. How was I to fair in a unique situation? Uncle Julian's checklist for meetings was a shocking single page. Unlike the 24-page instruction guide on how to maintain the fangs.

"I am very excited to meet them as well," I said as genuinely as I could. "Let head there now. "

* * *

The Goodight Meeting Room was located on the first floor. It was fairly close to my office. The tall burgundy doors didn't mute the momentous chatter from the other side. The line of increasingly distressed statues perfectly read my emotions. Much to my surprise, it was the only room that wasn't accessible through a secret passage. In essence, it was an impenetrable stone rectangle. An impenetrable rectangle I now had to walk through to get to the front.

Okay, just don't forget how to walk. Then, well, I'll figure it out.

"Are you ready, Miss Savio?" Betsy prompted.

I took in a subtle deep breath and smiled. "Yes. It'll be a simple introduction and overview."

Waiting any longer would raise suspicions. Time was on

my side, but first impressions were a coin toss. If my voice wavered, if I tripped over nothing, or if I didn't radiate the proper confidence in my abilities, it would leave me with a bad standing with the overall staff. Betsy was already a tremendous help, or rather, she felt responsible for minimizing any of my screw-ups. But the rest of the Head Staff? I had yet to properly interact with them.

With gusto, I pushed the doors open. The long walk to the front looked like a trickster oasis in a desert. The staff's heads all turned toward me as I gathered my courage and strutted down the aisle. It was oddly easy to do. My slight heels clacked with purpose. I could feel their numerous stares. An abrupt silence enveloped the room.

Don't trip—don't trip—don't trip—don't trip.

The three other Head Staff members were at the very front. Betsy trailed behind me as quietly as she could. The excessive smiling nearly made my face twitch with effort. With each step, a fury of butterflies formed a tornado in my stomach. As I neared the front, a massive presentation board blinked to life. The handbook's details flashed across my mind.

Step 1. Greet.

"Welcome back to 7 Moons Hotel!" I said as evenly as I could.

A muffled collection of greetings echoed back to me. My eyes scanned the staffs' collective surprise. Some looked unbothered while others looked like they were about to combust. Of course, my entrance was worthy of such a reception.

"I'm sure you heard of Mr. Savio's vacation for the winter," I started stiffly.

"Yes," the staff collectively agreed.

I turned to face them, positioning myself beside the presentation board. My knees trembled as if my muscles were replaced by jelly. Tension threaded by shoulders much like the glossy decorations of my uniform. My mouth went dry at the sight. The meeting room was crowded like a small concert. A concert for a person who has never sung before. My forced smile ached, but I made sure to move on to the next step.

Step 2. Run down plan.

Thankfully, Uncle Julian left a word-by-word paragraph for me to repeat. To my relief, the presentation board moved automatically.

"My name is Avira Savio and I… I will be the one running things here until the Spring Solstice." I tried to sound confident, but the slightest waver in my voice betrayed my intention. "T-there will be no radical changes so just do exactly what you have planned in your individual and…and overarching schedules. Any changes will be closely discussed with the Head Staff."

I stole a glance at the Head Staff. Partial relief peppered by sentiments. They all nodded and smiled in approval.

"Let's have a great grand opening," I said enthusiastically. "I will be doing exactly what Mr. Savio did. Whenever you need me, simply come find me or send someone or call me."

Step 3. Wait for applause.

The silence in the room amplified my uncorking nerves. Did I sound convincing? I must have been a peculiar sight to them. Just last week my uncle stood before them. He likely had an amazing pep talk and there I was, staring back at them with a twitching smile.

"Yeah!" someone in the far corner shouted. "Let's have a great grand opening! I have many cars to park and brooms to align! Are we dismissed, Miss Savio?"

Her voice echoed loudly, much more than my own.

"Yes," I said a bit bewildered. "Yes, you are."

An explosion of applause followed. Relief was only a momentary bliss. The day that awaited me would be… a worthy challenge.

6

A Normal Guest?

By the time I made it back to the lobby, the greeting staff had assumed their positions. They moved like clockwork as I struggled to find my bearings. Yes, I was aware the hotel was fully booked, but I didn't quite assimilate what that would look like. The astonishment on my face nearly gave away how oblivious I was to everything. My eyes could hardly keep up with the movement. Nothing short of a spectacle was awaiting the guests.

I gulped down my brewing nerves as I took everything in. A small orchestra floated above my head. Dancers in elaborate costumes lined the walls that weren't occupied by staff. Water Manipulators had their hands ready, large spheres of water floating around them. A red carpet was rolled to perfection. The multitude of heads could be seen through the large colorfully stained windows.

Griffin emerged from the elevator and jogged toward me. The day had just begun and he already looked exhausted.

"Miss Savio, great meeting," he said as he caught his breath. "We have a small group of VIPS here first. They're our most loyal guests so they're really looking forward to this."

"Honestly, me too," I admitted stiffly.

Griffin frowned slightly. "Did Mr. Savio tell you what you're supposed to do?"

I badly wanted to nod in agreement.

"No," I replied slowly. "It wasn't mentioned in the handbook."

Or presentations for that matter, but I kept that bit to myself.

"When the presentation is over, all you have to do is greet the first guest. Shake her hand and give her this." His gloved hand pulled out a silver key.

I hesitated. "This may be a dumb question, but is that…"

"No, Miss Savio, it's not, I can assure you. Lady Monica is fond of how silver glimmers, that's all. She has the imperial suite on the 2nd floor and requested a key instead of a card."

"Interesting choice," I muttered.

"Eh, she's just weird. Staying at a vampire hotel and requesting a silver key is ridiculous, but Mr. Savio indulges her," Griffin grumbled, offering an elbow to me. "Follow me. You have to stand in the center as the doors open."

"Do I have to say something?" I asked quickly.

"Just smile and give a quick speech of welcome," Griffin instructed.

I nodded, spiders of anticipation crawling up my back. Griffin guided me under the grand chandelier. From where I stood, I could finally make out the silhouettes of many heads. Griffin assumed his position behind me. He noticed my gaze and granted me a small smile. His stiff posture mirrored my own. My hand grew clammy as my eyes fixed on the moon-shaped clock. The slow-moving hand gradually met the hour. The faintest tick fueled my enveloping dread.

"Positions everyone!" Betsy's voice called. Although I

couldn't see her, she was very present. "Band! Get ready for 7 Moons Awakening!"

Waiting for the doors to open was like squeezing an overfilled balloon. As the large clock ticked closer to the grand opening. A sudden urge to run raided my senses. The moment of truth was upon me. I had to be the best possible Hotel Manager. I couldn't be bad at the job. I simply *couldn't*. Would my wit and handbook be enough? Besides my problem with Cromwell, I had the success of the grand opening weighing on my shoulders.

A whole year of preparation...

"It's time!" Two doormen appeared at either side of the towering doors.

The grand doors swung open. A crisp breeze pushed through with the precise motion. The band started playing as a tidal wave of guests flooded the lobby. The dancers jumped to the center, bursting into an elaborate dance number. The water manipulators greeted every guest with their own sphere of water. There were so many things going on, I didn't know what to focus on. Laughter and astonished gasps filled the band's deliberate pauses. Lights flashed as confetti exploded above me. An incredibly sweet smell floated in the air. The band moved back to their original position. The water manipulators took back the spheres and began to juggle.

Was I still in the hotel or was I transported to a circus?

As the show finished, the faces of the crowd became clearer to me. Many eyes lingered on me. Some of the older ones searched for Uncle Julian. I cleared my throat as silence fell.

"Hello everyone," I said with a stiff smile, my mind searching for words. "T-thank you for being loyal guests and for joining us during the grand opening."

The guests didn't react to me. They just… stared.

Griffin moved beside me. "This here is Miss Savio, she will be replacing Mr. Savio for the winter. Rest assured, she is the best possible replacement and will surpass Mr. Savio's managing standard."

A pinch of relief speckled my uncorking nerves.

"Ah, yes." An elegant old lady emerged from the crowd. "A young manager is what this place needs."

Her words changed the crowd's reaction instantly. The array of guests was as diverse as 7 Moons proudly claimed to be. Ghosts stood beside goblins. Half giants poked above the crowd. Low level witches and mages stood proudly, their magical pendants shimmering. Werewolves laughed with skeletons. The humans that entered were much more ecstatic about a new Hotel Manager.

I quickly realized who she was. I loosened my grip on the key. Lady Monica's silver dress shimmered. Light danced across the floor as she walked toward us.

"Lady Monica," I greeted, extending my hand. "Thank you for your kind words."

Griffin had underestimated her affinity for silver. She was dripping in the forsaken metal. I tried not to inch away from her. There was no verifying if what she wore was real. Much to my relief, only her right hand was bare of any jewelry. Her bright red lips curled into a smile. From the looks of it, she was human. A very interesting human.

"Nonsense," she replied. "No need to thank me. I only speak the truth, whether people like it or not."

I maintained my smile. "Your imperial suite is waiting for you. I hope everything is to your liking."

"I'm sure it is." Lady Monica's deep green eyes met mine.

"Now, tell me one thing, Miss Savio. The hotel will continue to run as usual, correct? No previous activity has been halted?"

"To my knowledge, nothing has been stopped. Only improved," I reassured, extending the key to her. The amount of silver she had was starting to fry my nerves.

"Good," she said, grabbing the key. "I hope you also enjoy your stay at 7 Moons Hotel, and good luck. You may need it."

Without saying another word, she marched toward the elevator. The rest of the guests followed, speaking to the greeting staff and walking to the front desk. A sigh escaped my lips as the crowd fully dispersed. My knees became a cowardly jelly. I silently thanked Griffin and the rest of the staff. That could have gone… incredibly worse.

DING.

The 7 Moons cellphone jolted in my pocket. I nearly flinched at the jerking motion. My hands were still clammy from the grand opening, but I managed to open it. My eyes focused on the glowing notification.

EMERGENCY:
LEN JEVARD PORTRAIT & STAFF ALTERCATION
RED LADY LOUNGE
HELP IMMEDIATELY

"What?" I exclaimed loudly.

The lobby suddenly grew quiet. Everyone's attention shifted toward me.

I bit back a cuss at my stupidity. "Oh, sorry, I just… looked at the weather."

Before anyone would prompt a further conversation, I stiffly walked away. My mind flashed back to the map. Red Lady Lounge was a considerable walk from the main lobby. With guests and staff circulating, dashing to the lounge would raise alarm. I… I needed to take the secret passages. A blend of excitement and dread waltzed as I walked to the right wing. If I remembered correctly…

As the thought connected, my eyes locked on the towering green flower vase. I dashed to it and pressed my hand against the burgundy wall. A square indented, giving way to the inner wall. For a moment I couldn't believe my eyes. As I slipped in, my mouth parted in awe. The secret passages appeared like deliberate halls. Although a bit narrow, it was lit by a warm, steady light. The wooden floors were spotless, though a bit cracked. Many questions blimped to life. Did all 7 Moons Hotel have secret passages? Were they all so well kept? From my understanding, all of the passages were interconnected.

I pulled out the map and found my location. My eyes repeatedly traced the directions.

"Run straight, up the stairs, and turn left," I muttered to myself.

Without wasting any more time, I surged forward. My steps were quiet as I raced up the narrow stair. The left turn made my feet nearly skid. My eyes locked on the covert exit. A latch glimmered under the low light. I quickly yanked it and barreled into the room. I didn't pay attention to the lush red lounge. My eyes fixed on the odd scene.

Two staff members held onto the third. The third was halfway inside the painting. The portrait's frame jumped, cracking the wall that contained it. Incoherent shouting filled the lounge. I could barely make out the spew of cusses.

"HOW DARE YOU?" the voice inside the painting shouted. "I'LL SHOW YOU WHAT AN ORIGINAL PAINTING CAN DO!"

"What's going on here?" I blurted out.

The staff's head whipped toward me. "HELP! HE'S GOT HAROLD!"

I ran to them and grabbed Harold's legs. With a forceful yank, we all went flying onto the deep red carpet. Now that I could see the painting clearly, I suddenly understood why Uncle Julian bolted the paintings rather than simply hanging them. Deep cracks brought a cloud of white dust to the red carpet. The painting suddenly met my eyes. His glowering anger abruptly stopped. He reached out, adjusting his name, and froze in his original pose.

"Hey!" the gray-haired man screamed. "You coward! Now that Miss Savio is here you're gonna act all innocent!"

I slowly rose to my feet. "What… What the heck happened here?"

They lined up, all avoiding my questioning gaze. "Sorry, Miss Savio."

The blue-haired woman cleared her throat. "Len and Harold have old beef and today things got out of hand. That's all."

"That, and all of the paintings have been acting weird," Harold grumbled.

Just as I was about to talk my phone buzzed again. Dread wrapped around my shoulders at the sight.

"Alright," I said, glancing at the new notification. "Let's get working."

* * *

The hours blended together. Daylight faded into a dark hue. The hectic buzz of foot traffic became a ghostly remnant of the day. Exhaustion stormed the castle that was my endurance. I found myself leaning heavily on the counter.

56

Was it professional behavior? No, but my ability to care was nowhere to be found. My face was squished between my hands. Having the slightest frown was somehow more comfortable. The lavish scents of the lobby grew ghostly to my nose. My legs were like cinder blocks. If day decided to breach the night before I slept, I feared I would have to resort to crawling. 436 out of 437 rooms were filled with happy guests. The lack of people before me was almost comforting.

Few staff members were stationed at their posts. Griffin, my lobby mate, was as zoned out as I was. We were all awaiting the same thing. The last guest. Room 321.

My eyes were fixed on the slowly ticking clock. The gentle sound filled the silent lobby. It was much more pleasant than the jarring ding of the cell phone. I could almost hear it behind the sound of my thoughts. Placing it on vibration was a risk I wasn't willing to take. My mind looped around Cromwell's hidden plan. With every move I made, the chances of me getting a one-star review grew slimmer. If things continued to move in my favor... Then things would be alright?

Something twisted around my hopeful conclusion. I was no magic wielder to have a developed intuition. My gifts didn't lie in psychic prediction but a different type of ice distilled into my being. It was present since the moment I arrived. That sense of impending doom I couldn't quite shake off. Was I misinterpreting exhaustion for doom? Unlikely, I wasn't that dramatic.

Then what was it?

I straightened away from the counter. With a slow blink, I glanced at the computer monitors. The guest's check-in was expected a minute before midnight. Perhaps staring at the security cameras would help time move faster? Staring at the clock was making my mind buzz. By implementing a 13-number code, I had access to the majority of security cameras. Would staring at halls be entertaining? I was partially hoping it wouldn't be. Miscellaneous entertainment was fun for guests. Not fun for Hotel Managers.

However, that didn't stop me. The massive grid of cameras blinked to life the moment I pressed enter. At first glance, it was a whole lot of nothing. Guests strolled the halls, few collected in and out of Red Lady Lounge and Pinicle Bar. Events officially started the next day. None of which required my presence. Yet as I randomly clicked, a blinding flash suddenly hooked my attention.

"Hm?" I muttered to myself, my eyes lingered on the camera's identification.

Third floor. Warcaster Hall.

I amplified the small square to a bigger rectangle. The night was crystal clear. An electric storm wasn't forecasted. I would have seen the lightning flash from where I stood. My brows pushed into a confused frown. The hall looked empty. All I could see were the numerous statues and tiny paintings. But as I brought my face closer to the screen, something subtle moved along the wall.

"Hey," I prompted my lobby mate. "Do you see anything here?"

Griffin jolted at the sound of my voice. Without hesitating he followed my gaze. His tired expression turned into a strained concentration.

"No? I just see the hall?" Griffin said slowly. "What do you see, Miss Savio?"

That was the very thing I asked myself.

"I think I may be delirious," I said jokingly. "But I do see something."

I clicked off and went to the corresponding camera. No matter how hard I tried, I couldn't distinguish what crept along the corner. A ghost? No, the figure wasn't solid enough. 7 Moon Hotel cameras were designed to capture the supernatural with ease. Plus, there weren't any resident ghosts. Was it a passing shadow? That didn't explain the flash. Was it—

The massive doors swung open with a strong bang. My gaze whipped away from the computer. The entire staff stiffened as if an invisible odor turned them into statues. An intense cold filled the lobby. A cold that went far beyond skin and bone. The lights wavered as an overloaded broom slowly glided through the door. About ten suitcases were balanced and carefully tied to the rich brown broomstick.

The luggage boys jolted at the sight and vanished without touching the luggage. Even Griffin took a small step back. Trailing behind the overloaded broom was the guest we all awaited. The soft sound of her heels filled the lobby. I forced a smile to my face, but it didn't reach my eyes. I wanted to fully observe the individual that made the staff stiffen. The pleasant environment turned into a cold tundra.

The mysterious witch finally stepped in. She seemed to be around my age. Her caramel-toned hair made perfect donuts tracing her forehead. She wore an elegant long-sleeve and a fanned-out skirt. Her eye-shaped earrings glittered with every step she took. Her feet were nearly as quiet as mine. Impressive, given the type of heels she wore. However, as she grew closer, I finally met a pair of calculative eyes.

Subtly, she surveyed the vast lobby. Her gaze bounced swiftly from various points of interest. Not once did her eyes stall on the meticulously planned allures the lobby provided. Her expression didn't shift away from her perpetual neutrality. Was she impressed? Did she like the renovations? Both of those questions didn't matter. It was as if she brought the winter's all-encompassing coldness with her. Even with the charm's protection, I could *feel* the tug only magic did to reality.

"Welcome to 7 Moons Hotel," I greeted politely, trying to keep my voice cheerful.

Griffin backed into the drawer as she reached the desk. Her gaze met my name tag, then shifted to my eyes. I fought my smile's urge to crumble. The warning bells in my mind became a thunderous ringing. The moment our eyes locked, my impending dread made covert sense. The cloud that hovered over my conclusion thickened. I could suddenly understand the staff's reaction. The witch's eyes were a remarkable shade of purple. Dazzling to the innocent gaze, but a different type of coldness hovered closely to the surface. Not a single speck of warmth adorned the intricate purple. Even her friendly smile managed to silently threaten the hotel's order.

How odd was it for me to feel that way over a stranger? Evidently, her presence had more meaning than I was aware of. The entire staff was aware of it. Nobody went near her as if they were previously ordered not to. Why didn't I have some notice? Was I supposed to offer special treatment? Who *was* she?

The witch extended her card without saying a word. The card was unlike the ones I had seen throughout the day. The 7 Moons Hotel logo was matte against the deep burgundy. As my hand met the cool plastic, a yellow spark popped between us. I withheld a flinch and carried on with the routine check-in. Sparks with hotel cards weren't natural. Nor was the numbing chill that crawled up my arm. However, I wasn't concerned. The charm would give a blatant warning if it was a bewitching spell.

"I see there's new management," she said matter-of-factly. Her voice was lighter than I expected.

"Yes, this is only a temporary arrangement," I responded formally. "Things will continue to run the same way or better."

I swiped her card across the scanner. The ding flashed two windows of information across the screen. Griffin quickly handed me a blue card. The room number glittered under the warm light. I stole a glance at her name and history of stay.

Membership: Platinum
Stay Number: 121
Name: Miss Caine
Duration of visit: 7 days
Cost due: Free
Reason: Accumulated Reward Points

"Well then." I cleared my throat. "Miss Caine, you booked room 321 for 7 days. If you need anything, do not hesitate to contact the front desk."

Instead of handing it to her, I slid the card across the counter.

"Thank you, Miss Savio. Oh and, no need to reprimand the luggage boys. They know I like to bring my things up without assistance."

"Noted," I answered stiffly.

Truly, reprimanding the staff wasn't on my to-do list. I was thinking something like a gentle interrogation. My encroaching exhaustion had momentarily pulled away. As the elevator door closed and Miss Caine left, I turned to Griffin. The intricate cold gradually pulled away, leaving only a remnant of the chill.

"Griffin," I said lightly. "Mind explaining?"

"My answer won't satisfy your curiosity. Mr. Savio told us a very long time ago to limit our interactions with that young lady." Griffin sucked in a sharp breath. "He personally handled any request she had, which wasn't often. If I may, I suggest you stay away from her as well."

"Huh, interesting," I muttered.

He was right. I wasn't satisfied with that response. If the circumstances were different, perhaps I would have done more. Yet the thought of doing anything else that night brought exhaustion to the shore of my mind. The day was over. I just wanted to retreat into my room and *relax*.

"Well, pardon me for the rest of the night," I announced. "I have other very important business to attend to."

7

A Task For One?

It wasn't often the fine line between dreams and reality morphed together. Rather, it wasn't often I ever saw anything other than a perpetual darkness. A different type of confusion submerged my vampiric senses into a deep fog. The darkness dispersed, giving way to a crumbling arched entrance. A large sign was slanted, and faint lights traced two words:

Lomir Theater.

It wasn't a familiar setting by any means. However, I moved with a strange familiarity. I was there with a purpose. A purpose that was hidden from my mind but not my body. My movement was obeyed, yet restrained by a series of invisible strings. Almost as if my presence forced its way through a thick molasses. An inconsistent pressure pushed against my shoulders. The false world rippled with every step I took. As strange as it seemed, my feet didn't quite meet the cracked marble tile. I... glided over it?

The once-grand theater unfolded before my eyes. A true shell of past grandeur greeted me with a thick silence. Deep stone walls towered high above me, leading to a triangle-shaped ceiling. Sparse moonlight trickled in through the angular cracks. Sharp pieces of wood decorated the faded red carpet. Rows upon rows of red seats rippled. Statues blinked to life in the seats. With each step I took, another set trailed behind me.

My eyes were pulled to the brightly lit stage. Velvety blue curtains were pulled back. The strong stage light acted like a second sun, searing the details into my eyes. The setup was an… office of some sort? A false window flashed as if a storm raged behind it. A desk was placed in the center, mostly empty besides a single leather book. Two doors were on either end of the stage. One was a deep, glittering purple, the other was an unnerving yellow.

An intricate stillness hugged the stage. My eyes were locked on the purple door as my body beckoned me closer to the stage.

What is this?

The sound of my thoughts was a distant whisper. My true emotions were covered by a thick veil. Yet… I could feel something. Two pulls in opposite directions. A raging fire and a withering cold. I could feel…*someone.*

The two doors flung open. The loud silence was punctured by the screech of the hinges. My mind grew silent. My thoughts were forced behind an impenetrable dam. My eyes bounced between the doors. The darkness was nuanced. The subtlest motion gave way to someone. With a simultaneous clack, the shadowy figures stepped out.

Both of their forms were covered in darkness. I could barely make sense of their silhouettes. A girl stepped into the office. Her movement was muffled by her precision. My mind buzzed as I tried to make out any more details. My vampiric senses electrocuted my need to run.

Is this a show? Why am I here?

The girl's form solidified into the silhouette of elaborate garments. Her dress fanned out dramatically. Her large hat spanned out at an angle, slicing the wall as she drew closer to the desk. On the other side was a taller shadow. His long beard contradicted the angular edges of his suit. The presence I felt finally focused on the two figures.

It was far too powerful to belong to any human. Far too intricate, far too… tumultuous. No matter how much I wanted to pull away from the feeling, my senses were magnetized to it. But how? Why?

I need to stand—I need to leave.

My will was no longer obeyed. My eyes were glued to the stage. Darkness encroached on the corners of my vision. The contrasting shadows met at the center. The desk served as a measly divider. My mind buzzed like a frenzy of wasps. All I could do was wait for the show to start.

"I've told you numerous times." A deep distorted voice escaped the taller shadow. "Do not involve yourself in my affairs."

"Involve myself?" the lady said, her voice equally as distorted. Her light tone was frosted with bitterness. "This is far past my mere involvement. This… this is just the beginning of the end for you. The beginning of my—"

An ironic chuckle bounced off the walls as the man threw his head back in amusement. "Wrath? Is that what you wish to call it? You make a mockery of magic by calling this that. All you're doing is meddling as a way to get back things that are unobtainable. You know that very well."

The tall shadow moved closer, silence spreading between them like a descending tornado. The cold dread swirling within me seeped deeply into my stirring consciousness. The pressure upon my shoulders amplified, pushing far past my natural senses. My soul… My soul nearly trembled as the man's shadow grew taller. Looming over everyone and everything, I watched him gather the encroaching darkness. One by one, the statues around me began to crumble. The jarring sound was muted by a slow-moving silence.

"You'll regret ever crossing paths with me." The lady's distorted voice trembled. The slightest shake in her voice resonated with the crumbling building. She looked tiny in comparison, but I could feel every fiber of her anger expand and dig like sharp thorns.

"You'll regret it," she repeated. "With each spell, with every damn breath I take, I will make sure you have no peace. I will be the splinter that finishes you off for good."

"The only thing I have ever come to regret was sparing you." The man's shadow had engulfed the entire theater. The festering darkness repelled away from me, yet my skin prickled with an everlasting chill.

"Just wait," they said in unison, the sound of their voices acting like a shock wave. The world around me began to tremble. "Watch as your reality crumbles."

"Just wait," they said louder.

The shaking intensified. As if a warrior slashed through fabric, tears of light took over my vision. The closest seats succumbed to the darkness. I wanted to leave. I wanted to get up. Yet, my instincts pointed to a different conclusion. The pressure continued to force me into the seat. The spreading silence made the air ripple. The show wasn't over.

"And you." The towering shadow pointed straight at me. "You stay out of it."

The shadow surged forward like an eagle to a small prey. The dream began to crack like a mirror. Blinding lights seeped through the tears of reality.

CRACK.

My eyes snapped open. The chaos of the dream rattled my mind as I sprung out of bed. I nearly crashed into the wall. My hands curled into tight fists. I whipped to see the empty room. Shadows danced across the walls. The wind blew a citric scent but I could feel the passing breeze. Where was I? Did I fall into another dream? Was I in the hotel?

I couldn't find my bearings. The ground had a ghostly tremor. One that followed in heed of a giant's steps. The thunderous crack echoed like a thousand warning bells. It sounded far too real. As if lighting struck an unsuspecting pole and shook the building's entire foundation. Impending doom circled my instincts, nearly short-circuiting my senses. I could feel every single movement in the hotel. Constant tugs in every direction made me realize I was fully awake. I quickly pulled away. My hand hastily swiped the light switch on. My chest heaved as if I had run a marathon in my sleep.

"What... What was that?" I muttered shakily.

I didn't have enough time to ponder the situation. My stomach sank the moment my gaze met the deep crack. A spidering crack plagued the once smooth ceiling. I blinked rapidly, were my eyes playing tricks on me? Was the thunderous noise true to reality?

"The ceiling..." I said slowly, my thoughts crawling to a dreadful conclusion.

The 5th floor. The Restricted Area. The one place no one was allowed to enter was... breached?

No, it couldn't be. It simply couldn't. The mere notion

threatened everything I struggled to maintain. What if what I felt wasn't just a nightmare? My eyes repeatedly traced the jagged crack. Pieces of paint subtly rained onto my bed. The division between floors wasn't thin. If something fell, it wouldn't have produced such a monstrous crack.

I forced myself to focus past it. Clarity pushed through the fog of my thoughts. I found myself marching toward a dangerous conclusion. What if the dream… wasn't a dream at all? What if what I felt was happening in the Restricted Area? What would that mean for the hotel?

The handbook didn't have a section for Restricted Area breaches. I glanced at the glimmering red button. With a single touch, the entire hotel would go under lock down. Undoubtedly, that would alert every single guest of an unknown danger.

I glanced at the crack once more. My eyes traced the frighteningly deep groove. There was one thing I knew for sure. Something happened on the 5th floor. Something… or *someone*. I didn't have the luxury of a false alarm. If there was a danger, I had to deal with it quietly. How? No idea.

"No, don't be hasty," I said to myself. "What would Uncle Julian do?"

His awfully cheerful voice drifted to my mind.

"I left a handbook in your room so if you have any questions, don't call me."

As thorough as the handbook was, it didn't cover emergency plans. Well, besides the basics. The basics were mostly common sense. I had to think rationally. I took a deep breath and marched to my nightstand. The glossy black phone was on, but no one called. If the staff was aware of something, the phone would be blaring. If I were to alert them… It was the logical move. From my understanding, Onyx would still be in the hotel. A simple hint to the unfolding situation was the best move.

Without hesitating, I called him. Pacing around the vast room, I gathered my thoughts at the sound of the dial. Within three rings, Onyx's monotone voice answered.

"Miss Savio," he answered.

"Onyx, don't alarm yourself, but I want you to be very alert and notify the others of any suspicious movement around any 5th-floor entrances," I said as evenly as I could.

Silence met my reply.

"Onyx? I—"

A sudden knock at my door interrupted me.

"It's me, Miss Savio." Onyx's voice cut through the door and echoed on the phone.

I quickly opened the door. I didn't expect him to arrive so soon.

"You got here quickly," I stated the obvious. "That's good. Well, I'll cut to the chase, come and see for yourself."

Without turning around I pointed to the ceiling. Confusion flashed across his gruff face. All six of his eyes flickered between the ceiling and I. Far more times than it was necessary.

"I don't understand," he said slowly. "What am I supposed to be looking at?"

"Huh?" I responded. "The crack of course—"

As I spun around, my eyes met a smooth ceiling. Not a single crack or imperfection. I blinked, surging deeper into the room.

"T-There was a crack in the ceiling! A— A huge one!" I explained, nearly tripping over my words. "I don't understand..."

I swiped at my bed. A fine dust coated my skin instantly.

"See." I showed him my hand. "This is from the ceiling!"

His head tilted to the side. "Miss Savio, with all due respect, if you just wanted someone to talk to, you can just say that. That looks like powdered sugar, it's far too uniform to be debris."

"But…"

"Please trust when I say, I pride myself in my work. These eyes don't miss a single thing. Nothing has happened. I can gladly put my hands in a flame and I won't get burned."

I looked at my hand. Sure, it was compact and nearly identical to sugar, but I saw what I saw. That was not a figment of my imagination. However, with the proof vanishing before my eyes… Convincing Onyx would be futile. The look he was giving me made me realize one thing. I was not Mr. Savio. I was his 21-year-old boss with a stained record.

"I see…" I muttered. "Just… don't ignore my request. Please."

He nodded slowly. Without saying another word, he vanished in a thick puff of black smoke. I turned back to the ceiling.

"You're playing tricks with me," I spoke to it, my glare deepening. "Little do you know who you're messing with."

The dream's conversation drifted to the shore of my mind.

"Stay out of it,"

"If you're threatening my reviews, I will not stay on the side lines. Mark my words."

Quite daring of me, yes, but I couldn't risk simply ignoring. I had already ignored too many things. The subtlest peculiarities weren't a factor of an overactive imagination. With every turn I took, there was something covertly calling my attention. From the flickering lights to the angry paintings, to the crawling shadows. Were they all coincidences? Or were they all warnings? Perhaps I wasn't overthinking then. Perhaps I really was onto something. But what?

8

A Spectrum of Shades?

Determination blazed any flowering hesitation littering the garden of my mind. Waiting was for fools, especially given the circumstances. I was already a fool for pushing my instincts aside. If the ceiling was already playing tricks on me, then what else was in store? What else was happening in the rest of the hotel? Were people blind to the shifts in reality? At least someone else had to have noticed something, *anything.* Some loose thread I can pick up and thoroughly investigate.

However, this situation was… intricately different. I was basing myself on a dream. A dream my mind scrambled to keep intact. The ghostly sensations still tainted my senses. I had to think of a proper approach. Nose diving into the unknown was fun, but it had to be incredibly calculated. My first move was obvious: The 5th floor.

For once, I found myself wishing Uncle Julian had added an extra chapter to the handbook. The entrances may have seared into my memory, but the rest was unknown territory. A frenzy of questions stormed my mind. Too many questions, and not enough foreseeable answers.

I quickly switched out of my pajamas and threw on the uniform. I made sure to secure the beads in a stylish bow. It was my only defense against medium levels of magic. That was the only explanation for a "healing" ceiling crack. A magic user of some sort was on the 5th floor, hypothetically speaking. Be that as it was, I could no longer feel the distinct sensation. No raging cold or fire. Just… emptiness.

Without waiting any longer, I snatched the small phone and charged to the door. Before my hand met the cool metal knob, I glanced over my shoulder. The night was darker than most. But most importantly, the ceiling remained impeccable. A bitter taste blossomed on my tongue. A tease like that was a declaration of war. But with war came little battles. The first of which I seemingly lost. But… who was my supposed foe? And what was I fighting? Or attempting to fight, rather. One thing I knew for sure, only the sharpest of wits would claim victory.

I silenced the storm of questions. Any type of investigator needed a clear mind.

I have to assess the situation thoroughly. Just like with Armeli's Chalice, minus Cromwell's intervention.

The nearest entrance to the Restricted Area flashed across my mind. My first target: Olet Statue. The warrior statue was a tough object to move, but with determination and vampiric strength, I would easily find the latch. The door's hinges squeaked slightly as I peered into the Alterin Hall. My eyes traced the hall meticulously. For a moment, it was like I stepped into another dream. The velvety red carpet… rippled? Yes, that's exactly what I saw. The carpet had the rippling effect of a gentle wind across a pond. Beyond that, every piece of decor was tilted. Portraits on the walls were off-center. Statues were facing toward me rather than away.

I usually didn't pay attention to the subtle details of the decorations. Yet this time, this time the statues etched expressions spoke. Did they speak a ciphered language of… danger? I took a ginger step forward, the ground was buoyant against my feet. My only comfort was the fact the doors remained as they were intended. Straight and tightly closed. My eyes flickered to the multiple cameras. Icy dread slithered across my chest.

How are they not seeing this?

There were many answers to that question. One of which being magic. However, such a simple answer entailed many things. 7 Moons Hotel's cameras were not susceptible to magic. It was Uncle Julian's pride and joy, second to the hotel itself. If magic managed to bypass such a sophisticated system… Then what was I getting myself into? I was tempted to call Onyx again. But, my instincts decided against it. If the anomalies disappeared once again, a negative staff review would be a fire raging against dry bushes.

Taking in a subtle deep breath, I glanced at my watch: 3 am. Most guests were asleep or partaking in other activities. I wouldn't have to worry about guests stumbling into my unfolding situation until 7 am or so. That meant I had to work fast and as quietly as possible. If I wanted to solve the problem by the break of dawn, then I had to be efficient in my approach.

Hasting my pace, I sharply turned the corner leading into the main hall. Electric butterflies zapped my stomach as I spotted the statue. Unlike the rest, it remained untouched. The Olet Statue stood tall, casting a long shadow across the rippling carpet. His sharp spear glistened menacingly under the flickering warm light. His shield was placed by his feet, dull in comparison.

I blinked a few times. The constant rippling made disorientation a threat. The usually cool air shifted to a humid warmth, making the sleeves cling to my skin. My dark hair already stuck to my forehead within seconds. Time was of the essence. Although I was protected by my charms, there was no telling how much they could withstand. And more importantly, how much *I* could withstand.

My hand met the smooth marble base. With gentle maneuvering, I pushed it to the side. My gaze locked on the carpet. It was surprisingly lighter than I expected it to be. Or perhaps I underestimated my strength? As I shifted further to the left, a piece of the carpet clung to the base, tearing a purposeful cavity. Instantly, I noticed the lackluster leather strap.

"Perfect," I muttered, stealing a glance at the ceiling.

The strong contrasting sensation was ghostly to my senses. Whatever caused those feelings had either moved farther into the 5th floor or left by another exit. Either way, I had to ascend into the Restricted Area.

I swallowed down my uncorking nerves. I reached for the strap, my hand barely meeting the leather. Instantly, a searing pain sharply bit into my skin. I yanked it back. Staggering back, I crumbled to my knees.The instant burn slashed me. My skin festered as if I brought it across a branding steel. My vision blurred. My ears rang like a siren running corner to corner.

Silver. Silver powder.

"Fuck," I said through gritted teeth.

I bit my bottom lip, withholding a scream. My teeth nearly punctured through my own skin. It was a pain like no other. My entire body buzzed with only the smallest burn.

Adrenaline flooded my veins. My senses amplified and dulled simultaneously. How could I be so careless? I didn't notice it under the dim lights. No matter how fine, there was always a subtle sheen. A sheen I completely overlooked.

Did I fall into a trap? Was someone about to appear behind me? I knew something wasn't right. I should have known something was waiting for me. If anything, it was a confirmation. My dream wasn't just a dream. Two individuals were feuding and I was now involved in it. The dream was a warning. A warning I possibly received too late. It was a clue of some sort. Barely a corner piece to work with.

I brought my hand close to me as I took several deep breaths. The effects of silver exposure would last longer than the pain. I had to—

RING. RING.

I jolted at the abrupt sound. My phone buzzed in my pocket, my stomach sinking instantly as I snatched it out. It was the customer complaint line? I couldn't just ignore the call. I had to answer no matter how many dots danced across my vision.

"Yes?" I said as evenly as I could.

"Good evening, Miss Savio. I hope I didn't disturb your sleep," The unknown staff member greeted me.

"N-not at all." My voice strained slightly. "Noise complaint where? Fourth floor?"

"Third. Warcaster Hall, room 322..." her voice trailed off. "Are you okay? You sound a bit..."

"I stubbed my toe, that's all," I lied. "Room 322. Guest name?"

"Liam Lanst. The complaint came from neighboring rooms. Loud grunting and constant banging were reported."

My frown deepened. "Fighting?"

The line went quiet. "For your sake young Miss Savio, let's

say it's fighting."

Oh.

OH.

Oh no.

"I see. I'll head there now," I responded, my voice wavering. "I-Is there any other complaint I should know of? Perhaps thunderous noises or weirdly behaving floors?"

"Nothing else has been reported, Miss Savio," The unknown staff confirmed. "But if anything does come up, I'll contact you immediately."

My mind flashed back to Lady Monica.

Could she have...

"Has Lady Monica gone to the 4th floor?" My voice shook.

"No. Lady Monica has stayed in Red Lady Lounge."

"I'll be off then," I said stiffly.

The unknown staff hung up first. I gripped the phone tighter than I needed to. The constant ache was nearly dizzying. The warmth of the hall became feverish. My cheeks were flushed as I took in a shaky breath. I avoided the sight of the burn. My healing factor wouldn't be enough to fully aid me. I...I would have to push through it. The searing pain was slowly numbing. Good for the moment; terrible for long term.

The 5th floor had to wait. I had to deal with the complaint first. If I allowed more time to pass, I'd have bad reviews to worry about. I just wished the first complaint wasn't so... awkward. Interrupting such things could also lead to bad reviews. And worse, I needed to talk to the guest.

Slowly rising to my feet, I walked to the elevator. I decided to avoid the secret passages. What if the other entrances were laced with silver? Either my foe worked quickly or there was more than one person to worry about. My mind raced quicker than my feet. Everything was unclear. Far too unclear for my minuscule comfort.

The elevator dinged as it arrived. I stepped in and quickly pressed the third floor. The pain in my hand had subdued. Dots no longer raided my vision. My body still buzzed, but it was manageable. As long as I didn't move my hand, I could function. Even the touch of a small breeze spiked the pain.

My mind grew quiet enough for me to notice something. The elevator music became an odd mix of pieces. Indistinguishable to my ears. Almost like a bunch of tunes smashed together by an amateur DJ.

Dread crawled across my chest like a dozen spiders. Just knowing the guest's name wasn't enough. I needed more information. I quickly put his name in the database. The phone trembled in my grip as I read.

Liam Lanst.

Warlock.

3 day stay.

Solo booking.

First time stay.

Whatever activity he participated in usually required two. I wasn't sure whether to feel awkward or afraid. Perhaps both? All I could feel was the chilling tremble that settled in my body.

The elevator doors opened with a cheerful ding. Instantly, a striking frigid breeze struck me like a blizzard. My breath became visible in the air. Shadows clung heavily to the walls, creating a thin path for me to walk on. I could barely see the thick outline of doors, let alone the room numbers. The moment I stepped into the shadow-filled hall, my charms began to glow. I charged forward. The darkness repelled away from me.

The room number lit faintly in the darkness. Warcaster Hall was to the left of the elevator. Whatever was happening, I had to quickly find a way to put an end to it. But how? My thundering feet were silent against the rippling carpet. Any sound was muted beside a shrill creaking noise. My ears strained to hear any sound reminiscent of the complaint. I could only hear my thoughts. How was I to solve a magical problem? I was not magical by any means.

My eyes darted from door to door. Room 322 had to be the last suite in Warcaster Hall. Warning bells roared. A familiar feeling flooded my senses. The same tug and pull ignited in my chest. My eyes locked on room 322. I focused my attention on the overflowing sensation. Beneath it all was something else… Something purposely evasive. As if… as if it knew I was looking it.

I swallowed down the crawling panic. I needed to get in that room. Without hesitating, I dashed forward. As my hand reached, time slowed. My instincts took over. The door exploded like a bomb. Sharp shards of wood shot across the air. I lunged to the side. The shadows dispersed in an instant as if the sun blazed each one out of existence. A thick white smoke spilled out of the room like a dragon's charged breath. The intricate feeling under my senses vanished with the blast.

I sprung to my feet, kicking away the stake like pieces of wood.

"Mr. Lanst!" I called, my voice piercing through the enveloping silence.

I swatted the smoke, and the buzzing of my beads dimmed. For once, I could hear someone move. Anticipation gripped every fiber in my body. A serpentine ice circled me as I stepped in. Did a bomb go off? Debris littered the once-clean ground. Deeply grooved cracks lined the floor. The air had the faintest glimmer as if someone sprinkled glitter. I could feel the indistinguishable swarming sensation. The incomparable feeling of *magic*.

Pure energy itself.

I couldn't see past the smoke yet, I could barely distinguish a kneeling figure.

"Mr. Lanst?" I prompted slowly.

As the smoke finally cleared, my eyes fell on someone else. Kneeling on the floor was not Mr. Lanst. Kneeling on the floor was no one other than… Miss Caine.

9

A Mirror of Smoke?

Everything made sudden sense. So much so that I forgot how to talk. I could only watch as Miss Caine slowly rose from the floor. Her staff was tightly clenched in her hand. The bright purple crystal glimmered menacingly under the moonlit room. With the smoke clearing, I was finally able to see the damage around me. What I saw at the entrance was a taste of the true destruction room 322 endured. The burgundy walls had gaping holes as if someone had been thrown into them. Chairs and tables were broken in half. Only the mirror's frame was intact. Shards of glass littered the carpet like false stars.

Miss Caine didn't look any better. Her once prettily made up-do had become a hectic half-do. The caramel donuts of hair had miraculously survived, but the rest of her locks cascaded down her shoulders. Her fashionable dress was… chard? The edges had the unmistakable singe only fire could make. Her hands seemed to be covered in soot. The mere sight of it reminded me of my numb, silver-burned hand. I quickly tucked it behind me.

The unfolding scene before me didn't give me a black-or-white answer.

Where was Mr. Lanst?

I took careful steps forward, my eyes locked past Miss Caine's feet. Was that a…blob? Although mostly blocked by the witch, I could see needles for legs and a faint red glow around it. Yet beyond that, I noticed something peculiar. The ground around it was… mending itself? Before my eyes, the cracks *filled.* Just like the ceiling in my room.

Dread pooled in my gut. Was she the one in the Restricted Area?

For the first time since I entered, Miss Caine's icy gaze met mine. Pure bewilderment must have been plastered across my face. She moved the staff away from me, but not entirely.

"What…" I trailed off.

There was so much going on I wasn't sure where to begin. With my voice dimming, I took a long look at Miss Caine. That fogging sensation…

That feeling…

It collected like a swarm of magnetized icy particles to a stray bit of metal. Just like the dream, a blizzard found its way to my chest. Only the contrast was gone. Gone, yet lingering in my senses.

I turned away from her for a moment. To my relief, nobody crowded the doorway.

"Miss Caine," I started again, this time finding my voice. "What *happened* here? Where is Mr. Lanst?"

"So you're not with them," she said suddenly.

I blinked. "I'm sorry what?"

"Your hand, Miss Savio," she stated, her voice even. "You were burned by silver and you're hiding it."

My hand was tucked behind me. I had only given my back to her for a split second. How did she…

"That doesn't answer my question, Miss Caine," I said carefully.

"But it does answer mine." She shortened the exaggerated distance between us and gestured to my hand.

I hesitated. With the charm, her magic would backfire if she attempted anything I didn't agree to. How could I know it wasn't a trick? To pretend to heal me but then magically whack me? Yet, as contradictory as it seemed, my instincts pointed to a different direction. Perhaps it was silver fogging my rational, but something crucial was missing. Something I prided myself in noticing.

Malice.

Even the most minuscule speck of malice was far from her steady gaze. A smile tended to hide people's true intentions. However, she didn't attempt to look friendly. Not even a wisp of a smile cracked her serious expression. Her steady hand didn't waver.

What harm would come in complying? My hand was entirely numb. A headache thundered between my temples. The remnant effects of the silver were slowly encroaching as the adrenaline wore off.

I extended my hand to her. The mere motion made my jaw clench. I tried my best to keep a neutral expression. The wound was worse than I realized. Oddly, the warning bells in my mind had gone silent. I didn't quite trust the charismatic stranger, but I didn't think she'd try something dangerous. For her own sake.

Her palm lit with a warm yellow light. With the other hand, she lightly touched my knuckles. Her touch was much warmer than I expected. Magic users usually ran cooler than most.

"Will you allow me to heal you?" Miss Caine asked, glancing at the beads. "I can't bypass the charm if you don't agree."

I nodded slowly.

Her glowing hand hovered over mine. Pins and needles raided my skin, a cool relief showered the wound. Before my eyes, the burn mended. The fogging blur pulled away from my mind in an instant. The headache dissolved with a wave of clarity. The golden light reflected cleanly off her cold eyes.

How… interesting. It wasn't often I had direct contact with magic.

"There." She let go. "The sight of it was bothering me."

"Right, thank you," I said stiffly.

The gesture was… kind, but kindness was often a facade. With my mind clearing, I started to see what I was missing. What I needed was a proper deduction of information. The mending chaos around me provided a few answers, though incomplete.

Liam Lanst was nowhere to be seen. Besides Miss Caine's distinct presence in the room, there was a dimming blob on the cracked floor. Was I to assume Mr. Lanst was the blob? To my recollection, Mr. Lanst was a warlock. Not a blob with needles for legs.

My gaze shifted to Miss Caine. The sensation she stirred was a confirmation. There was more to that dream than I initially wanted to believe.

"You understand I have many questions and I'm in need of answers." I started.

Miss Caine sighed in annoyance. "Your uncle was much more hands-off on my business."

"Uncle Julian and I are very different people," I clarified.

"Oh, that much I'm aware of," she said bluntly.

Her staff began to glow, but she directed it to the blob. With a forceful strike, the blob turned to ash. The motion was so nonchalant I wasn't sure what to do. If that truly was Mr. Lanst, then did that mean—

"I was incredibly wary of your standing, given your abrupt arrival." Miss Caine interrupted my thoughts. "A hotel management punishment is not what I expected to find. Let alone all of your petty helping of citizens. But, I was pleasantly surprised to see your name on Armeli's Case."

I frowned slightly, trying to hide my intrigue. Who was this girl? Those things were classified to some extent. How could she know of Armeli's Case? Let alone my eccentric punishment? Did those things become public information? Or did she too share my habits of breaking into Cromwell's office? If that was the case, Cromwell *really* needed to upgrade his security system.

I didn't answer immediately. Much to my surprise, our expressions mirrored each other. With silence thickly spreading between us, we entered a quiet showdown. I had to choose my words carefully. Clearly, I entered a battle of wit. But most importantly, the determining factor. Was she an ally or a foe?

Allowing her to believe I was naive to her situation was dangerous. I couldn't just blink at her. I needed to show that I too had forbidden knowledge. Knowledge so closely held I didn't know what to make of it. What I was about to say was incredibly risky.

"I can't deny that," I started slowly. "What I'm trying to understand is who regrets sparing you so badly. And if that has anything to do with what's going on in 7 Moons Hotel."

I resisted the urge to gulp down my crawling anticipation.

Miss Caine's stony expression didn't shift. Yet, she also didn't answer me immediately.

Ironing out the wrinkles of dread, I turned my focus to the wrecked room, attempting to pinpoint anything I missed. The floor was mending itself. Just like the ceiling, everything shifted back to place with a low rumble. The ground had a subtle vibration. It wasn't a function of her magic. As etched in stone as her expression was, magical strain always made itself present.

"How do you know that?" Miss Caine asked, her voice dangerously low. The iciness in her purple eyes could have brought a blizzard over the desert. Yet I couldn't allow my gaze to waver.

Stand on business or you're screwed.

"Seems to me like we both have our ways," I replied. It was more of a bluff, but I needed information. "Something is going on here and I need clear answers from you, Miss Caine. If your research of me was thorough then you'll know I will not leave if this isn't resolved. *Completely* resolved."

Miss Caine's frown deepened, but she moved her staff aside. With a gentle wave of her hand, a creme-toned business card materialized.

I gingerly took it from her. Were my eyes deceiving me? Even with the lingering darkness, the words nearly taunted me. A… detective agency? Ghostly excitement sprinkled through my apprehension. A case had fallen upon 7 Moons Hotel. And I… I could be very involved in solving it. Who could stop me? I was the Hotel Manager of 7 Moons. I could—

I quickly stopped the flood of nonsensical thoughts. The mere notion was fogging the potential severity of the situation.

"Well, Miss Savio, I will try to be clear enough," Miss Caine said firmly. "This is a business stay. What you witness here is me taking care of business."

Before I could ask for more details, she continued. "I'm after the Oldera Amulet. That green blob, now ash, was an Illusion Shifter. One of three. The Amulet spawns three as it searches for grounding material. Which I'm preventing."

I nodded slowly. Her words made sense in terms of language, yet, I had no idea what she was talking about. Damn my lack of magical knowledge! I needed to grasp things within my intellect. My mind traced the previous occurrences. The rippling carpet, the slanted doors, and the twisting decor. Were those all illusions? How was that possible?

"And you tracked it here?" I asked gingerly. "How?"

"How much do you know about this building, Miss Savio?"

A dangerous question evading my own. In full honesty, the history of the old hotel did not have a file in my memory. I knew the building itself was very worthy of the label "old" but its exact origins were a mystery to me. Uncle Julian bought it way before my birth.

"The ins and outs, yes, the origin? Not at all," I admitted.

"Understandably," she said lightly. "This building is well maintained but it's over 200 years old. It has a proper magical rooting system and that's what the Amulet needs."

"And this Amulet," I retraced her words. "What does it do exactly? Who's the holder?"

She hesitated. I could visibly see her weighing her options. Whether if it was a good idea to tell me more information or not. But, if she truly processed the information she read about me, then she would know I wouldn't be leaving so easily.

"I can answer one of those questions," Miss Caine started. "The Amulet is a Time Warper. It grants the user two time jumps. One to the past and one to the present. I'm sure you're well aware that messing with time is not natural."

I had to agree. Time was never to be messed with. "So this… *blob*, is taking energy from the magical rooting system. A glorified termite, that's what I'm understanding."

"Indeed," she agreed. "The Oldera Amulet just needs one fully charged shifter to reactivate. It will be very obvious when that occurs."

"I see…" I processed. "And Mr. Lanst? Did the Illusion Shifter get to him?"

"That blob was has the essence of Liam Lanst, but it's

certainly not the real man. These things can absorb the essence of people if their current disguise is considered… compromised. Which makes finding and capturing them in one go extremely vital."

My stomach dropped at the notion. The Illusion Shifters could absorb essences? I was so worried about reviews I didn't realize something important. I needed the guests to be well if I were to get reviewed. I couldn't have guests disappearing.

"Oh…" I trailed off.

"Yes, so you see, that's my business," Miss Caine replied. "I'm sure this explanation will suffice your insatiable curiosity, Miss Savio."

She said something else, but I missed the last bit. My mind was too busy connecting the dots. The corner pieces of this new puzzle dawned.

"That's why I saw the cracks in the Restricted Area…" I muttered to myself.

Miss Caine's eyes widened at the last bit. "What? You saw another crack? In the 5th floor?"

"You know about the 5th floor?" I asked quickly.

"That's beside the point. Answer my question."

I bit back my initial response. Sometimes there were things more important than necessary sass. Only sometimes.

"Yeah, I was tracking it," I responded. "But I lost connection after the silver incident."

"Track? As in… you can *sense* the damn thing?"

"Vaguely, yeah. It's subtle but annoyingly present. Like a splinter."

"Thank you for the information." Miss Caine grabbed the staff. "I must go then."

"Oh no, you can't," I interjected.

The idea of joining another case was exhilarating, but now it wasn't optional. I *needed* to. It was my duty as Hotel Manager to keep the staff and guests safe from threats. Whether it was a wrong order or a magical issue, it had to be fixed.

There was far more at risk than my reviews and Cromwell's cryptic plan b. The entire hotel could crumble. The people could start to go missing. That jeopardized my uncle's entire hotel enterprise, and from my understanding, the present as we knew it.

"Just because I told you the details does not mean I require your help. Your input was enough—"

"These people are under my care and I demand you take my help," I spoke as authoritatively as I could. "Clearly your method of finding these things isn't as accurate as mine."

"And how would you know that, Miss Savio?"

"Well, Miss Caine, you said it yourself. You had no idea there is an Illusion Shifter in the Restricted Area. I'm sure you, as much as me, don't want to have the Amulet activated or the guest disappearing." A daring smile tugged at the corner of my lips. "You have to take my help."

Her stare threw daggers at me. Yet, I didn't yield. The Oldera Amulet Case had to be solved. It simply had to be. For more reasons than my petty little punishment.

"You sound more excited than authoritative, Miss Savio," the Witch Detective said after a moment.

"Take it as you will, but in this case, I have to have my way."

It was clear I wouldn't take no for an answer. I didn't take Miss Caine for a fool, and denying my help would be just that, utterly foolish.

"I prefer solo endeavors, but it seems we're forced to work together in this situation," she remarked bitterly. "I don't fair well with the constant input of imbec—individuals."

"Understandable," I agreed.

"I will make myself very clear Miss Savio, I am the Detective and you are the delinquent Hotel Manager. Tracking the Illusion Shifters is what I need from you. You leave the rest to me. Do you agree?" Miss Caine extended a steady hand.

I would be the fool if I didn't. Although I didn't really like the way she phrased it, I'd find a way to bend our agreement. For the greater good, of course. Much like I did with my role as Anonymous Helper.

"I agree," I said confidently. "The Amulet will not be activated. That much I can assure you."

I shook her hand firmly and smiled. She returned the smile. Although it wasn't warm or friendly, it was a sign of a mutual agreement.

The Oldera Amulet would not be activated. The guests and staff weren't going to be harmed. And whoever was after the Amulet, they would be stopped.

But before that, a few calls were to be made. I still needed to get coupons for the poor neighbors. Even in dire situations, customer service always came first.

10

A Worthy Plan?

It was shocking how much unquestionable authority I had. Within minutes, a selected handful of staff came to room 322. The three people unit had a militaristic vibe as they marched down Warcaster Hall. Not a single word was exchanged as they worked. One placed the door and screwed it in. Another collected the sharp pieces of wood and cracked them into tiny, nonthreatening chunks. The last one slid coupons under the nearby doors. I knew it wasn't proper to stare, but I couldn't look away. It had pleased me to see every possible mishap had a crew to take care of it. But, I expected to receive some sort of questioning glance.

Were exploding doors a common occurrence in 7 Moons?

"Is that all, Miss Savio?" Patricia, the emergency carpenter, asked.

I looked at the door. The work was impeccable. It would be hard to believe anything took place in Warcaster Hall mere moments before.

"Oh wow! It looks great!" I exclaimed. "That's all for now. The inside is in dire need, but let's take care of that another time."

"As you wish, Miss Savio," Patricia replied.

As the unit turned away, a necessary prevention came to mind.

"Oh, and will you do me a favor please?" I called after them. "Don't mention this to a single soul."

The unit collectively nodded. I couldn't help but wonder what went through their minds. Nobody openly questioned my story about Liam Lanst and the destruction. I had already prepared a perfect story to satisfy any questioning thought. It was a simple tale, really. Mr. Lanst could not contain his drinks and had a bit of a rampage in his room. For which he decided to apologize and leave. I found it to be quite convincing.

Now that the door was put together, I turned my attention to Room 321. I took in a subtle deep breath. Such a smooth progress of action was not awaiting me. Stealing a glance at the time, I had about 2 and half hours before breakfast began.

Miss Caine had retreated into her room before the unit arrived. Although, the use of the word "retreated" wasn't entirely proper. Without much effort, I could feel her icy presence lingering behind the door. Was she looking through the door's subtle peephole? Most likely. I was tempted to stick my tongue out, but given the circumstances, I withheld my antics.

I lightly knocked on the cool door. Without waiting a second, the door swung open. She had somehow managed to clean her appearance in such little time. Her hair no longer looked like a bird's nest. Her entire attire had changed from wrecked to a pretty deep blue dress. The soot that stained her hands was gone. Even her staff seemed to have had a polish.

"Alright, that's all taken care of," I began. "Let's take the passages up to the Restricted Area."

Two birds with one stone. I could inspect if any other entrances were tampered with.

"I was just about to suggest that." Miss Caine walked past and gestured me to follow her.

Her confident strides led to the beginning of Warcaster Hall. Her hand pressed against the burgundy wall with careful precision. I watched over her shoulder as her fingers traced a pattern. With a gentle click, the panel sunk into the wall, giving way to a new space. Confusion and intrigue waltzed together. No matter how much I tried to remember, that particular passageway wasn't listed on the map.

How...

"It'll be quicker through here," she said nonchalantly. "No silver powder, if you're wondering."

"You ..." I mustered. "How much do you know about the passageways?"

"I'm sure you're aware of my number of stays," she responded.

"122 stays, including this one, but that doesn't answer my question, Miss Caine."

"Miss Savio, connect the dots, will you? I don't think people would willingly stay in a hotel with such high criminal activity."

Again, she dodged my question and made another pop in its place. I decided to save my new question. Although, my sour expression gave away my simmering annoyance. Criminal activity and 7 Moons in one sentence? 7 Moons was usually a bore. The Oldera Amulet Case was an exception in my eyes. But, Miss Caine had a point. If she was a Witch Detective and her stays in Uncle Julian's hotels were numerous...

I pushed the thought aside. Such a thought was best served when the hotel wasn't in imminent danger.

"That's not my fault," I said carefully. "I've been a Hotel Manager for… 30 hours?"

"I'm just glad the hotel is still standing. Not that it's crumbling would have been your doing. For now, anyway."

Silence fell between us as I peered within the secret passage. Most secret passages were interconnected. However, the one Miss Caine casually showed me was distinctly different. It was lit by an unwavering warm light. No dust clung onto the deep wooden corners. The inner walls were clean and subtly decorated. The ground was polished wood, with only the slightest cracks. A gentle smell of strawberry lingered pleasantly. It made sense, given how close we were to the elevators.

"Follow me, Miss Savio," she said over her shoulder.

I tried not to jumble my mind with more thoughts than necessary. I needed to remember every silent step Miss Caine took. And more importantly, I needed to pinpoint that evasive feeling again.

Would the illusions reappear? My eyes traced the inner walls meticulously. Nothing warped or rippled. The natural sounds of our feet were a subtle pitter-patter. Unheard through the walls, but evident to my ears. The silence of the inner walls gave me a moment to process my approach. What went through Miss Caine's mind was a mystery. A magical approach was always distinctly different from a vampiric way of doing things.

Unlike Armeli's Chalice, I didn't have a convenient board of information. Thoroughly handpicked by Cromwell himself. I had torn bits of knowledge. Few things were evident enough. I needed to keep staff and guests safe. Illusion Shifters only obtained essences if they felt exposed. Miss Caine and I would have to find them and seize them within the same time frame.

If one of them slipped away… the damage would be irreparable.

As my thoughts crawled, the ground became an uphill slant, leading to sparsely placed steps. Each step reminded me of the hidden portion of a theater. A fly tower and grid, but only the ascending stairs. The metal supports looked feeble at first glance. However, that didn't yield Miss Caine's stride. If anything, it seemed routine for her. I wasn't sure how I felt about that. I pushed the thought aside and focused on our next move.

"Miss Caine," I prompted, my eyes avoiding the long drop beneath me. "When I find the Illusion Shifter, what's the plan?"

Her pace did not slow at my question. "That's all you're going to do. I'll do the rest."

My lips tugged into a slight frown. "With all due respect, what does 'the rest' mean?"

"Magical problems call for magical solutions."

So simply put. Yet, it didn't answer my question. However, I understood what she meant. It was a very polite, "stay out of it." That's exactly what I wasn't about to do. I had no way to properly assess Miss Caine's magical abilities. But, no matter how cruel it might sound, it was not sufficient. The state of the room was enough to see she barely won. How would she fare with another threat so soon after? Although I didn't have magical abilities, I would be a great assistance. I had to propose something more.

"I know I agreed to our deal, but you're not going to like me for this," I started, carefully putting one foot over the other.

"A correspondence of friendship is not my concern," Miss Caine replied evenly.

Her words made what I had to say easier. I was nearly grateful. Nearly. Were all detectives such… *asses?*

"Well, then, Miss Caine, want to know why I came down?" I asked, my tone becoming playful. "You were unable to conceal the threat. I got multiple complaints and the state of the hall was nightmarish. If that is your idea of containing these things, you will have to reconsider."

She turned around swiftly. "And what might you suggest, Miss Savio?"

I halted my step and smiled. For a moment, I nearly forgot we were standing on very feeble stairs. A very fun plan blimped to life. There were things the Witch Detective overlooked. Things that only a certain type of individual could scheme and pull off.

"A good old infiltration," I said confidently. "Use me as a decoy. The Illusion Shifter's magic can't get past this charm, can it? If it focuses on me, then you can do what you do best."

Her scowl didn't fully yield. "The charm may spare you for a bit. It's not impenetrable."

"I understand that, but that'll give you time to do your magic, won't it?" I offered.

Miss Caine paused. "That'll work if we encounter an individual, yes. If not, then…"

She looked above me as if the answer floated in the air.

"I don't know what I'll find," she said, nearly muttering to herself. "This is why I act alone, Miss Savio. Less variables more concise decisions."

"That's why detectives have partners, don't they? One pair of eyes tends to overlook some of the more… obvious things."

"Do not have a partner and won't have one, that I will assure you, Miss Savio," Miss Caine said swiftly. "But, it pains me to admit, you do have a point. If the circumstances paint itself like that, I'll consider it."

For her to consider something so soon was progress in my eyes. However, it might have been her way of shutting me up. Either way, I was excited to see the situation unfold. Fearfully excited, I might add.

Without saying another word, she continued her merciless stride to the 4th floor. Much to my surprise, we met a blunt dead end. I frowned, but not at the lack of stairs or ladder. Beyond that, the once comfortable chill had morphed into something... different. An enveloping humidity had infiltrated the intricate space. With each step closer to the wall, an invading heat pressed against my skin. My uniform's pristine sleeves clung to me. Sweat framed my forehead almost instantly. The sensation nearly reminded me of a forgotten furnace. Such a distinct heat only a forgotten inferno could produce.

The once-lit inner walls were smothered in a scattered darkness. It took a moment for my eyes to fully adjust to the different levels of shadows. The sudden temperature change was not the only peculiarity to note. Something more subtle shifted. Something only I seemed to have noticed. The quiet tranquility repelled, giving way to a newfound stillness. The stillness I could only attribute to waiting. A festering anticipation for something to happen. But... what?

Well, this is a clear indicator. The Illusion Shifter should be around... But why can't I trace the feeling?

I glanced at Miss Caine. She too had gone silent, but her attention was fixed on the wall. Minuscule cracks ran up the faint pink wall and shot straight up. From where I stood, I couldn't distinguish where the wall ended and the new floor began.

"Hang on a sec, Miss Caine," I said, keeping my voice an

appropriate whisper. "I need to check something."

Miss Caine nodded at my request. The evasive sensation was ghostly, yet familiar to me now. If the Illusion Shifter was close by, then I should have been able to pick up something more than the indicators. Anything. No matter how sparse.

I closed my eyes, plunging my vision into a steady darkness. My brows furrowed in concentration. What I needed to do wasn't entirely familiar territory. My past schemes never required such intricate tracking of individuals. Sure, my father made sure I was trained in my *one* skill, but I was no master. Even if it pained me to admit. I tried my best to push any clouding thought to the edges of my mind. I needed to get the Illusion Shifter closer on my radar.

Let's see... Where is it?

I forced myself into a restricted maze of presences. Several individuals blimped to life, yet their sensations were extremely faint. A sharp cold overpowered nearly every person's presence. Miss Caine's presence made my mind play an intricate tug of war. I needed to sense *past* her. I needed to gingerly expand my radar. A headache simmered under my effort. The cold pulled away from the foreground.

I forced my concentration past the 4th floor, targeting my radar to the 5th. I could no longer detect movement, yet the Restricted Area was within my grasp. Excitement simmered under my apprehension.

Where are you?

A sudden feverish spike stabbed into my senses. I latched onto the feeling like a desperate predator on an long awaited prey. Unlike before, the sensation was... sparse. Almost like a thick, smothering blanket on a horribly hot, humid day. In contrast to Miss Caine's magnetized blizzard, the sensation continued to spread farther than natural. An individual's presence was never more than a small radius. No matter how prominent. But this was no normal individual. With the feeling circling my radar, I could confidently confirm, the Illusion Shifter did not leave the 5th floor.

"I got it," I announced. "But it's different than before."

"Really?" Miss Caine asked, although she didn't sound as excited as I hoped. "That may explain the sudden heat wave."

I nodded slowly. It was very probable, which made me wonder a few things. Who could the Illusion Shifter be emulating? Some guests were… peculiar, but they never gave me the impression of a masquerading blob. And beyond that, what were the Illusion Shifters capable of? Did they have limits? Weak points? Asking Miss Caine would be like asking a wall. Divulging such information to me would cement my position in the matter. She made it very clear before. The Oldera Amulet Case was a solo endeavor. Although, I had to admit, I was quite intrigued to know what happened in room 322. What would a magical battle look like? How would *I* fare in one?

Miss Caine took a deep breath. Just as she did before, she precisely tapped the wall. The rhythm was simple, but each perfectly placed knock lit a square. Within seconds, several slabs popped out of the wall with a muted rumble.

"If the Illusion Shifter started draining, there would be more than a few cracks on the wall." Miss Caine started. "Seems to me, this Illusion Shifter is waiting for something. Or looking for something."

"So, we're still doing my infiltration plan?" I asked.

"Yes, Miss Savio. If the situation calls for such a thing," Miss Caine agreed half-heartedly. "The space between the walls will be narrower, but enough for you and I."

My eyes trailed up the ladder. It went higher into the darkness than I was comfortable with. Although it was perfectly clear, I still didn't like how high it went.

"Sounds like a plan then," I responded, tension slipping into my voice.

"Right, I'll go first," she said, her grip subtly tightening around the staff.

Miss Caine moved up the slabs with fluidity. One step after another, I could no longer hear her ascending. Her feet were silent as she climbed to the Restricted Area. I did my best to suppress my brewing nerves. I usually enjoyed a proper infiltration. Unfortunately, I found an electric butterfly nest was beginning to hatch.

I wiped my clammy hands on my pants. I wanted to believe that was a byproduct of the sweltering heat. My hands met the uncomfortably hot metal. With each step I climbed I felt like I was entering a furnace. The heat was amplifying dangerously with each passing minute. If we wanted to catch the Illusion Shifter, it had to be swiftly done. Yet, as I rose deeper into the shadows, my mind latched onto a dangerous fact I overlooked.

Hot places and magic users was not an amiable pair. If temperatures continued to spike, what effect would it have on our fellow Witch Detective? At first glance she didn't look particularly bothered. Just… slightly annoyed. Which seemed to be her resting expression.

As I climbed up to the platform, the shadows pulled away enough. The Restricted Area walls provided slits of light, allowing us to see just how narrow the space was and how far it went. Uncle Julian had the rest of the hollow wall filled. At first glance, it seemed to be the only covert entrance to the 5th floor. From where I stood, there was no way of knowing.

Clearly, I was unaware of the many things 7 Moons Hotel had to offer.

Miss Caine glanced at me, then moved to the space. She side stepped as quietly as she could. Critters scattered at her precise movement. The heat danced with the expanding sensation of the Illusion Shifter. Discerning the two different heats was becoming harder. My nerves were waltzing. I felt like an incredibly recoiled spring.

As I moved into the space, a pungent smell of rotting iron assaulted my nose. I made sure my movement was soundless. Each step was placed on the balls of my feet. Majority of the slits were below my line of vision. Yet, even the narrowest one acted like a torch. I could feel the heat more than I wanted to. The three piece uniform was starting to become a punishment to wear. Questions dared to derail my train of thought. Why did Uncle Julian need a Restricted Area?

Miss Caine brought a finger to her lips as she stopped in front of the only near eye-level opening. I watched as she bent her knees as much as the space would allow. Gingerly, she leaned forward. The warm light illuminated her brilliant purple eyes. The shadows across her face reminded me of an old-school western showdown. Her gaze darted from side to side. A subtle bewilderment invaded her face.

"This... This is not..." she muttered.

The sight must have perplexed her. Instead of completing her sentence, she grabbed by wrist and pulled me to the slight opening. She moved closer to the dead end, giving me enough space to see. Her hand was feverishly hot. Yet, concern didn't have time to settle in. My eyebrows raised in question. I leaned and looked through. For a moment, my mind struggled to process what I gazed upon. What I saw wasn't a room or a wall.

It was… sand? A room full of sand?

11

A Striking Puppet?

Sand? A room full of sand? I knew my uncle was a bit eccentric, but a massive sandbox? One thing was clear, that wasn't Uncle Julian's doing. The Illusion Shifter had certainly done something. But what exactly? Apprehension slithered between every fiber of my being. The slit's limited view restricted a proper assessment of the unfolding situation. Aside from the mounds of sand on the ground, I wasn't sure what I was looking at. Was it a hall? Or was it a huge room with no walls? The blasting heat made it harder to steadily gaze through.

I tried to bypass the physical heat and tried to latch onto the Illusion Shifter's presence. I could still feel a strange sensation, yet I still couldn't pinpoint the individual. The sensation continued to expand to a near dizzying extent. Without having an exact target, my plan of infiltration melted. We needed another approach.

"I guess we can just go in?" I offered, stepping away.

Although a bit hasty, from our position, I couldn't think of another course of action. Unless Miss Caine had some sort of spell? But given the situation, spell casting in a wall wasn't the most ideal. I assumed the Illusion Shifter had some sort of notion of our presence. Moving so blatantly into the Restricted Area had plenty of risks, but options were incredibly limited. As they usually were in such cases.

"The circumstances have changed, Miss Savio," Miss Caine said grimly. "It's best you leave."

My eyes widened. "What? I don't think—"

"With all due respect, you do not have the slightest clue about handling magical problems," she interrupted.

Before I could retaliate, she knocked her staff against the rough panel. The false painting frame flung open, heat slapping me across the face. Miss Caine's jaw clenched yet she didn't hesitate to step through. Without looking, she knocked the panel back. My hand caught it before it could shut. A wave of anger smothered my patience's dwindling flame. I didn't take her for a fool, but her actions were refuting that. How *dare* she? Only an imbecile would go in without any help. Just because she was the one with the title did not mean my presence was more of a hassle than an aid.

Magic users weren't built to withstand such a merciless heat. A summer day, yes. But a blasting inferno? Not at all. It was a known fact Miss Caine continued to disregard.

I watched her march onto the sand-covered floor. Her movements weren't as smooth as before. My mind flashed to the two instances I made contact with her. Her touch was already warm when she healed me. But when she pulled me to see, her hand was feverishly hot.

Is this girl crazy?

She was already exerting herself and she thought it was a brilliant idea to cast me aside? How dare she underestimate me? The hotel was at risk. The people were in danger. An unknown enemy was threatening the present itself. And now, her unwillingness to accept help was putting herself at risk.

Although I just met her, I preferred she wouldn't combust in 7 Moons Hotel and doom us all.

My brows furrowed in determination as sweat streaked my face. Not only was I not going to leave, I was going to be a *great* help. I pushed open the painting. Heat blasted against my skin as I climbed through. For the first time, the Restricted Area dawned before my eyes. The ceiling peaked higher than natural, allowing the night's stars to invade the hotel. Dunes in every direction and spanned as far as the eye could see. The 5th floor was completely wall-less.

As odd as it might seem, I no longer felt like I was in 7 Moons Hotel. Did I enter the Restricted Area? Or did a desert spill through an unknown portal? My feet slid with every step I took. I tried to look past the desert. The Illusion Shifter's sensation was intensifying, yet I couldn't see anyone. Were they hiding in the sand? The Illusion Shifter pinged multiple times on my radar. Far too many times.

Miss Caine turned sharply to me. "Miss Savio, if you jeopardize—"

My eyes locked on the farthest end. A subtle green glow was in the distance. Dim, but not weak. Without speaking, I pointed. Miss Caine halted her words and looked.

"There," I said clearly. "That must be it… but that's, that's not a person."

Miss Caine's staff began to glow as if reacting to her thoughts. Her eyes widened in a sour conclusion.

"This. This is a trap," she uttered. "An unavoidable trap."

As soon as those words escaped her mouth, the pings I felt

exploded into reality. The sand shot into the air and covered the only known exit. Two sand figures took form before my eyes. Each had a glowing core, and in the center was a nearly indistinguishable needle-like thread. The temperature sharply rose. Thirst began to plague my thoughts. I tried my best to push the notion aside.

My eyes bounced like a ball caught in a tight space. I took a small step back, my hands clenching into tight fists. Two sand enemies to fight. But how?

"This is why I wanted you to leave, Miss Savio," she said. Her voice had a sharper edge.

I shook my head. "Mine was just a warning. This, this isn't meant for you to walk away from. Like it or not, I'm not susceptible to heat like you are, Miss Caine."

Her scowl deepened. "The core. Aim for the core. Take it and snap it. Destroy these first, then go to the blob."

Without warning, she shot into the air with a bright blast. Gold tendrils exploded out of her staff as she dove straight to the nearest enemy. Like a whip snapping, one sand enemy turned to me. I flinched. Their flowing arms became piercing stakes. My mother's words suddenly flashed across my mind.

"It's best you don't underestimate how easy it is to get staked."

If only she knew the predicament I found myself in. Perhaps she would prefer Cromwell's mysterious punishment. Yet, even as I felt like I was about to melt, I… I still felt capable. I needed to be. I didn't have the option of failing. Miss Caine's jarring waves of magic boomed across the sand domain. My hands curled into white-knuckled fists. Sand kicked into the air. The tiny sharp particles made my skin sting. Sweat traced my face. Every muscle in my body became a tightly recoiled spring.

The moment had come. The showdown was mine to start.

Snap the core. Get to the blob.

Without hesitating, I charged forward. My instincts silenced my mind. A determined scream escaped my lips. Time slowed as a sandy stake sliced through the air. The sand beneath my feet shifted. The sharp edge barreled to my chest. I lost my footing. The tip sliced through the sleeve, clipping my arm. A tidal wave of sand flew into the air and crashed. The force shot me into the air like a ragdoll. Pain sprung to life as I crashed onto the mounds of sand. Black dots danced across my vision. The Illusion's presence and overbearing heat were making me short-circuit.

Miss Caine's magic lit the 5th floor. Thunder boomed and cracked. Light flashed and blurred at indistinguishable speed. The ground shook. The Sand Enemy stood still, waiting for me to get up. I gritted my teeth, getting to my feet. The glowing core taunted me. My limbs were starting to become like cement blocks. I scowled, ignoring the blooming pain.

"Get over here!" I shouted.

I charged with as much speed as possible. The Sand Enemy spewed attacks. Sand daggers sliced through the air. I dodged, shortening the distance. I just needed one clear shot. One shot and I'd snap the core like a twig. Tidal waves crashed around me. The Sand Enemy's efforts to keep me away weren't working. I could see the core clearer.

My hand shot out. The Sand Enemy collapsed into the ground and reformed away from me. I dashed toward it, but a wall erupted. I barreled through it, face-planting. The Sand Enemy shot back, farther from my grasp. I struggled to get to my feet. Thirst plagued my senses. Adrenaline couldn't keep the pain at bay.

How? How am I going to do this?

My muscles trembled. Sand caked my sweat-covered face. My mind raced faster than I could process. My vision was threatening to blur. A high-pitched ring sliced through my ears. I needed to do something. Figure out something. Anything. But what? I had to be missing something. The Sand Enemy was observing. Or perhaps it calculated a better way to end me.

My eyes darted to Miss Caine. She was slowing down, enough for me to distinguish her. Magic incomprehensible to my eyes exploded against the sand. Was she missing? I narrowed my eyes. No. She wasn't missing. The Sand Enemy was collapsing and reforming at the last second. Miss Caine wasn't even getting close... Yet, it wasn't making an effort to attack her either. Almost as if... the Sand Enemy was *trying* to make her exceed her limits.

Realization blazed through my exhaustion.

The task was *impossible*.

That's the point... It has to be impossible.

Anger exploded within me. The Illusion Shifter was using her logical mind against her. We... We needed to get to the blob first! But first, I needed to get to her.

I rose to my feet and darted to Miss Caine. The sand beneath me began to multiply, creating a steep dune. No matter how much I tried, I kept slipping. I slid back down and turned to the Sand Enemy. My eyes blazed with a fiery determination.

"Oh, I see," I muttered to myself. A weird smile overtook my angered expression.

A terrible idea struck my mind. I remembered how far I flew when a sand wave struck me. I needed to recreate that. Only then could I tell Miss Caine my discovery. I had to do it before it was too late. I took in a deep breath, the searingly hot air filled my lungs.

The Sand Enemy was getting ready to attack. The ground trembled. A sharp pillar began to take form beneath me. I bolted forward. The spikes trailed behind me, shooting into the air like arrows. Nearly within my grasp, it happened. A raging tidal wave blasted me off my feet. The force was like a speeding truck. The corners of my vision darkened as I sliced through the air. The ground sped to me. I crashed onto the hard sand. Pain exploded, yet my determination went beyond physical limits.

"Miss Savio?" Miss Caine exclaimed. "Goodness, you flew! Get out of the way, I'll take care of the rest."

The throbbing pain made it nearly impossible to speak. I grabbed her ankle, trying to get a hold of myself. If she vanished then it would be game over. I wouldn't be able to resist another tidal wave. I'd lose consciousness immediately.

"Wait," I croaked. "Don't attack!"

"What?"

"It's a trick!" I shakily rose to my feet. "You need to attack the blob first."

Exhaustion cracked her stony face. Realization crept into her eyes.

"That's why I couldn't get closer," Miss Caine said more to herself. "I... I don't have enough strength left for the launch and final blast."

I glanced over my shoulder. The Sand Enemies were multiplying across the horizon. We needed to act. Now.

"I can throw you," I said quickly.

Miss Caine nodded firmly. "Do it. I'll do a running jump."

I stepped back. She ran as my fingers interlaced. As she stepped, I flung her into the air with all of my might. Miss

Caine became a missile through the false sky. Her staff glowed, giving the appearance of a shooting star. The Sand Enemies charged toward me. Time slowed as I watched her soar. Her staff was lit with a blinding light. She struck the blob. Lightning flashed and thunder boomed. A sharp shock wave of cold air blasted the heat away. The sand disappeared in an instant. Cool relief flooded my senses. My knees turned to jelly, bucking me to the ground. Exhaustion slammed against me like a truck. My entire body ached, yet I found myself smiling through the pain.

"We did it…" I muttered. "We actually did it."

The illusion's remnants collapsed before my eyes. For the first time, I saw the true 5th floor. It truly was a wall-less floor without an endless ceiling. Chandeliers lined the domed ceiling. Intricate patterns ran through, enhancing the bewitching paintings of eras long past.

As the adrenaline subdued, every single strike I received blimped to life. A tremor settled in my hands and arms. My chest heaved as I tried to catch my breath. The cut on my arm stung. My sleeves clung to me. My side throbbed from every sand tidal wave. The Illusion Shifter's presence vanished, leaving behind an empty shell within my senses. I tried to get up, but I couldn't. I nearly wanted to lie down and take a nap.

I looked ahead of me. My head throbbed from the subtle motion. The distance between Miss Caine and I shortened. I could see her more clearly. The blob had situated itself in the farthest wall. Her back was to me, resting heavily on her still glowing staff. She slowly took a knee. From where I stood, I couldn't tell what she was looking at.

I tried to muster some energy to speak, but I found myself sinking into something else. A hauntingly incredible sensation distilled into my senses. It was almost enough to obliterate the aches from my body. That… *thrill*. That electrifying thrill of triumph. The notion alone gave me enough energy to speak.

"Miss Caine?" I called. "Did we succeed?"

Miss Caine didn't answer immediately. She slumped against the wall, taking a deep breath before answering.

"For the moment, yes. But…" Miss Caine trailed off.

"But what?" I asked, failing to get up.

"Things have gotten much worse," she stated, her tone oddly lighter than before. "Much, much worse."

12

A Moment's Delusions?

My triumphant thrill quickly dissolved. Much like Armeli's Chalice, the sweet taste of victory was fleeting. As much as I wanted to stay on the floor, I had to get up. My jaw clenched as I staggered to my feet. The jabbing pain in my side nearly made me fall over. The wound on my arm tingled, which was a good sign. The cut would heal quickly, and hopefully, without a scar. Walking toward Miss Caine, my feet made a heavy thud with every step. It was nearly hard to believe an entire desert had infiltrated the hotel's Restricted Area.

As my mind cleared, intrigue blanketed my thoughts. Why was there a need for a Restricted Area? Wouldn't it have been more profitable for Uncle Julian to use the space? There was barely any decor or anything notably important. Vast and dark, only the rising sun lit the grand space. The night was quickly succumbing to the day. I stole a glance at my cracked watch:

5:48 am.

How? Did time go faster? No way we were in here that long... were we?

I pushed the thought aside for a moment. Jumbling my thoughts wouldn't help me process the situation faster. Whatever the situation now was.

"Worse how?" I prompted, finally reaching Miss Caine.

She didn't answer immediately. She simply gestured me to sit before her. My eyes focused on Miss Caine. She looked nearly as disheveled as I did. But her exhaustion was more profound than mine. Although her expression remained neutral, a thorny strain distilled into her eyes. Miraculously, her unique hairstyle still survived the Illusion Shifter's trap. I wasn't sure which I found more impressive. Her magic? Or whatever hairspray she used?

I quickly sank back onto the ground. Sitting upright was nearly torturous. I eyed the wall as if it were the last drink in the desert. Oh, how I wanted to lean against it and take a nap. I forced the dubious thoughts out of my mind and focused on the situation at hand.

Miss Caine reached into her pocket and pulled out a thin, sparkling vile. It appeared to be a potion of some sort. Without hesitating, she uncorked it and drank it in a single gulp. A deep sigh escaped her lips, but energy visibly returned to her demeanor.

"Sorry for the delay. I genuinely couldn't muster another word," Miss Caine said, dropping the empty vile. "Just take a look at what's left of the Illusion Shifter."

I leaned forward as much as I could. The pain was slowly subduing to my relief. My confusion-speckled thoughts grew momentarily quiet. Before jumping to conclusions, my eyes locked on the incinerated blob. My brows scrunched at the sight. I wasn't sure what I was meant to see. All that was clear to me was the slight glow and… and a small needle?

I stole a glance at Miss Caine. Her eyes grew distant as her gaze fixed on the Illusion Shifter's remnants. Her expression darkened, contrasting the strong rays of sunlight dawning behind her.

"I… don't understand," I said slowly.

"Well, Miss Savio, I fear that if we don't find the last Illusion Shifter soon, we'll have other things to worry about," Miss Caine responded grimly. "That right there is a warning to the remaining Illusion Shifter. It'll try to ground itself permanently soon, and when that does happen… there's no stopping it."

My brows scrunched slightly. Several questions bloomed, pushing to the surface of my thoughts. Questions I finally dared to ask Miss Caine. My hands interlaced. My palms were still clammy. A pinch of tension settled between my shoulders.

"What *is* the Oldera Amulet?" I asked, keeping my voice even. "Don't take this as me questioning your methods, but why are you after the Illusion Shifters rather than the Amulet itself?"

Miss Caine blinked slowly. "The Amulet does not have one true form. Much like the Illusion Shifters, it can disguise itself as whatever object, become invisible, or do anything really."

My mind drew back to the strange dream. The overpowering presence. The man that spoke… Who exactly was he? Was he the one after the Amulet? Did that mean he was already a guest in the hotel? If that was the case, then Miss Caine would likely have attempted something to find him. Or prevent him from… something. Did I dare ask such a question? Even in her tired state, I doubted she let her guard drop.

I swallowed down my brewing anticipation, forcing the words to the tip of my tongue. "Who is after the Amulet? Who brought it here?"

Miss Caine's frown deepened. Hesitation made her lips

twitch as if she repressed her initial response. Or perhaps, those two questions asked the same thing?

"It's a twin Amulet," she answered gingerly. "It spawns where the other holder needs to appear in the present. It seems that he has already grounded his half of the Amulet, which is why the Present Oldera Amulet's Illusion Shifters are starting to grow in power."

I frowned. "Who is... *he?*"

"That is not of your concern, Miss Savio," she said sharply. "The prevention of his arrival is."

I sighed. Although her response forced the rest of my questions down, it provided some clarity. Miss Caine wasn't sent to prevent the Oldera Amulet's activation by a third person. She had assigned herself her *own* case. Whoever was stuck in the past was clearly her enemy. An enemy she didn't want to deal with. Truth be told, I didn't blame her either. The dream alone left me puzzled. I didn't want to imagine how it was to deal with the mysterious man in person.

"So, things are going according to plan?" I asked finally.

"Not at all," Miss Caine replied, her gaze fixing past me. "I was hoping for a 7-day window. I knew this 7 Moons Hotel was an excellent space to ground the Amulet, but I underestimated the Illusion Shifters's absorbing capabilities."

I looked around. At first glance, I couldn't see any imperfections in the area. The walls and ceiling looked impeccable. Yet as the sun fully dawned, several hairline fractures cracked the refined surfaces.

"Now with the last Illusion Shifter receiving a warning, our approach must be very calculated," she continued. "We can't be seen as often. Any suspicious glance can be interpreted as a threatening move. The Illusion Shifter will try to change appearances often and we can't have that."

Her words made my bruises ache more. "I still have my duties to do, so staying in my room is out of the question."

"Yes, staying in your room would indicate a plan of some sort," Miss Caine said more to herself. "Be sure to keep a strict tab on guests. Many may start to disappear if we wait too long."

"And the plan is? I'd offer but I don't know enough."

"You might not like what I'll say," Miss Caine warned.

"That'll make us even then," I replied with a slight smile.

She paused for a moment. "This plan is more reliant on your senses than I'd like it to be, but it's proven to be effective."

I nodded slowly. I didn't want to boast, but given it was my only ability, I sort of had to. "It's impeccable,"

"Well, yes, but that's not the only thing I need of you," Miss Caine started. "You must host a masquerade ball. As eye-catching as possible with the best musical entertainment."

"A masquerade ball?" I echoed. "When?"

"Tonight. 7 pm."

My stomach dropped like an anchor. "That's not a joke, right?"

"I did not develop a sufficient sense of humor for that," Miss Caine replied. "Let's hope we don't encounter more sand. I'm afraid I'll be finding it in places I shall not mention for weeks."

I was hardly concerned about the sand in her knickers. An alerted Illusion Shifter on the loose was hardly a comforting thought. The Oldera Amulet had plenty of tricks. Tricks even Miss Caine was inexperienced with. Tricks that bypassed my charm and 7 Moons's protections. Having a masquerade ball seemed to have more risk than reward. What if the Illusion Shifter decided to take essences? Would a mask be enough?

"Right," I said nearly shakily. "Then what?"

"I'll see as things pan out," she replied slowly.

That wasn't the response I was hoping for. If I wanted to make succeeding fathomable, we would have to work as a perfect team. As a unit rather than two moving parts. I had power in 7 Moons. She had insight. If Miss Caine were to decide to continue the case alone… There was no telling what the outcome would be. I would have to befriend the Witch Detective. Gain her trust somehow.

"How about we drop the formalities?" I offered. "You know my name already, so what's yours?"

Miss Caine's gaze fixed on me. She blinked as if she went through every possibility of granting me her name. I just hoped the good would outweigh the bad. It wasn't often I desperately needed to befriend someone. Perhaps if we were on a first-name basis, she would be more compelled to work with me? Or at least help offer more knowledge on the situation. Whatever insight I could get was more valuable than gold.

"Hazel," she said finally.

"Hazel," I repeated slowly, an odd smile tugged at the corner of my lips. Perhaps it was the exhaustion, but I couldn't hold back my response. "You're a witch… named Hazel. Well, your parents are very creative."

"Witch Hazel is much more effective at soothing than me. I can assure you that," she replied. I wasn't entirely sure if that was a joke. "Do not concern yourself too much Miss—Avira. Just arrange the ball and I'll give you a clear plan."

"Thank you," I responded stiffly.

For the greater good, I was about to throw off Betsy's hard work. If she knew the true circumstances, perhaps she would comply without taking issue. However, I couldn't tell her. I couldn't tell anybody. If someone were to find out—

"I should thank you," Hazel said suddenly. "I didn't realize the Illusion Shifter's game and I don't think I would have." She glanced at the tear in my sleeve. "You don't need me to heal you?"

I laughed slightly. Hazel's ego wasn't as high as most detectives I knew. Cromwell would never accept such a thing. Let alone admit it.

"My healing factor will do the job," I said with a tired smile. "Plus, I'd prefer you stop using magic for a bit. I assume combusting witches is a lot of paperwork."

Hazel rose to her feet and offered me a hand. The potion may have restored some of her energy, but there was still a slight tremble. I took her feverishly warm hand, my face scrunching at the effort.

"Well, I'm famished," Hazel said, dusting herself off. "Can you send a 3-course meal to my room please?"

"Will do," I responded. "How will I know when you come up with a plan?"

"Oh, you will know." The smallest smile appeared on her face. "Let's get out of here, shall we?"

13

A Will To Deny?

Hazel and I parted ways on the 3rd floor. She casually made her way down Warcaster Hall. Bits of sand trailed behind her with every step she took. Her demeanor was much more nonchalant than mine. Perhaps it was because she was the actual detective and I wasn't used to magical problems. I could hardly walk so slowly and carelessly. My power-walk was fueled by the start of Hazel's plan. The notion alone gave me a second wind of nervous energy. I power-walked to the elevator, my bruises aching with every rough step.

Staying in the secret passages had become dangerous. The last Illusion Shifter knew we were on their trail. How easy was it to lace every entrance? With magic involved, I assumed it was remarkably simple. Taking such a risk would be foolish of me. Aside from skipping the secret passages, I skipped my morning schedule. Now with an alarmed Illusion Shifter, I barely cared if the room didn't smell like their designated scents.

My morning priority: Speak to Betsy.

The mere thought sent an electric zap down my spine. Time

was ticking, but I wasn't concerned about a tardy arrival. I was more concerned about her reaction. How much could I say without endangering her? My appearance alone was alarming. That would provide some insight? Perhaps just enough for her *not* to consider resigning?

It's for the greater good. She'll understand? It's not like I'm crushing the spectacle she was planning for the past year.

Oh yes, that's exactly what I was doing.

The elevator dinged cheerfully at my frantic button pressing. The strong smell of strawberries nearly assaulted my nose. Although, the gentle bossa nova was a relief. Just earlier in the night, my ears couldn't distinguish anything. Thankfully, the amateur DJ had taken their night leave.

I slowly pressed the first-floor button and leaned against the wall. I could finally stand upright without wincing. The glossy gold doors reflected a distorted appearance. It packed an unsurprising shock I didn't have time to avoid. My hair was a mess. My uniform looked mangled beyond repair. Although I couldn't see my face clearly, I had a feeling it looked ghastly. However, Uncle Julian's appearance standards would have to wait a bit longer.

The elevator door opened, revealing the grand lobby. Several workers walked through the tall doors. A cool wind blew through, yet it didn't quite reach me.

"Good morning, Miss Savio," a few greeted.

Their many gazes glossed over my disheveled appearance. If they stole a glance, their reaction was far too subtle for me to notice. They simply went to punch in. I should have felt relieved, in some sense. But, the normalcy of it all was nearly jarring. 7 Moons Hotel's definition of normal raised a few questions. Yet, as quickly as they rose, as quickly as they were whisked away. The tall doors opened once again.

Betsy cheerfully walked in. Her vibrant smile and laugh filled the entire lobby. I tried to smile as her eyes met mine. As soon as our gazes locked, the smile melted from her face. Her lively pace halted abruptly.

"Good morning, Betsy," I said cheerfully, my lips tugging into a pained grin. "My office, please."

Betsy hesitated, her hand clutching her sweater. "Miss Savio, what… What happened to you?"

I didn't answer. I quickly turned around and gestured for her to follow. The walk to the office felt eternal as a stiff silence fell between us.

Just say what you need to say. That's all.

Betsy closed the door behind her gently. I decided to remain standing. Sitting down would prompt a conversation. Any sort of discussion of the true matter could not happen. I couldn't allow it. Tension interwove a tight web around my shoulders. I had to be swift and to the point. 7 Moons Hotel and everyone inside it depended on it.

"I'm sorry for this but…" My voice faltered. "But I need a masquerade ball ready to go by 7 pm tonight. The whole event has to be as enchanting as possible."

Betsy blinked slowly. "A—A masquerade ball? For… *tonight?*"

"I'm sorry," I said again. "I know this overthrows the Moonlight Strike Ball but I don't have another option."

Betsy didn't look me in the eye for a moment. She didn't answer me either. Her expression grew unreadable as her gaze traced my appearance. Suddenly each tear felt new. Each hidden bruise ached. The still healing cut on my arm stung as if it opened again. What if she refused? Then what? Throw the ball myself? Uncle Julian perhaps could manage, but me? I only knew it involved cool-looking masks. Everything else? I had no idea.

"Betsy?" I prompted gently.

The silence pressed heavily on my shoulders. She finally met my eyes. I couldn't decipher any of her thoughts.

"It'll get done," she said, her voice lacking any power.

A wave of relief crashed over me. Before I could speak, she swiftly turned around. The door swung open forcefully, leaving me alone with my thoughts. A strange emotion washed over my short-lived relief. Cromwell's annoying face flashed across my mind. I essentially just guaranteed I'd find out Cromwell's punishment. Yet oddly, I found that to be a desirable outcome. That meant we solved the Oldera Amulet Case.

I could already envision Betsy's report. *"Hasty. Impulsive. We want Mr. Savio back."*

My eyes traveled to the calendar. Two *x*'s marked the days as Hotel Manager. The third was now upon me and no matter what, I'll mark the fourth.

* * *

It would be a lie if I remarked how relaxed I felt. The wait was nearly torturous. After speaking with Betsy, I rushed to my room. I devoured my meal, took a quick shower, and ultimately decided against a quick nap. Even if I wanted to, sleep wouldn't come. The Illusion Shifter had done a number on my uniform. Which gave me a much-warranted intrigue. Who was the second Illusion Shifter? Who didn't return to their room last night? It seemed like I wouldn't get an answer until *after* the first check outs.

122

I remained at the front desk. The questions were louder than the vibrant activity. The ground vibrated with the stomping of numerous feet. Several people walked in and out of 7 Moons Hotel. As far as I could see, the preparations were going smoothly. Invitations were being slipped under the guests' doors. Betsy was nowhere to be seen and my phone had yet to irk my peace. I had a thirty-minute window. The perfect amount of time to do some investigating.

After a few minutes of clicking, I came across a conclusion I insinuated. The cameras didn't pick up a single thing. My gaze focused on the screen. The exact minutes and seconds were marked. The moment I fell for the silver trap was recorded in a frighteningly high resolution. However, no matter how many hours I backtracked, not a single person stalled.

I thought back to the sudden flash I saw. Yet again, I ran into a magical dead-end. Did I overestimate the hotel's magical resistance? Or did I underestimate the Oldera Amulet's capabilities? A blend of both was more probable. My nose scrunched at the thought. I really didn't know what to expect. I just hoped the final Illusion Shifter wouldn't bring another epic battle.

Our win was a pure whim. Much more than I would ever want to admit. Our next move had to be calculated and precise. What did that entail? Frustratingly, I had no idea. Hazel had a point in dismissing my initial involvement. Magical crimes required magical solutions, for which I had none. The Oldera Amulet Case was far more different than any case the Anonymous Helper undertook. There was hardly any magic involved. The stakes were minimal. The highest risk was getting arrested.

Yet as contrary as it seemed, there was an underlying thrill.

Deep within me, I was excited. A nervous buzz of energy strummed under the severity of the situation. Perhaps I was a bit of an adrenaline junkie. Or perhaps I had a few loose screws. But, no matter how much I thought about it, I didn't find a single ounce of regret. Inadvertently, Armeli's Chalice led to my next case. A type of case that had zero of Cromwell's involvement. It was as liberating as it was restricting.

I was assisting a Witch Detective. If Hazel's impending plan worked—

DING.

My phone jumped in my pocket. The small screen lit with a new type of notification.

A meeting request with guest 321 in Savio Office.

Decline or Accept.

I pressed the vibrant green button. Instantly, the elevator door opened. Hazel's icy presence distilled through. She looked much better than earlier. A pretty black long-sleeved shirt was paired with a fanned-out, olive-green skirt. Her hair was in a new high style, still sporting her signature circles. I suddenly understood why her broom was so overloaded. An outfit for every occasion was necessary. Not every detective had such bland attire.

Quickly, I made my way to the office. I walked in before her, situating myself on Uncle Julian's stiff leather chair. The office still smelled faintly of the chamomile tea I brewed earlier. It felt appropriate to have it in such a room. I wasn't much of a tea drinker, but I had a feeling Hazel was.

"Good morning," she greeted rather flatly. "I hope I didn't make you wait too long."

"I'm just glad it's over," I said, leaning back.

Hazel sat on the velvety chair and subtly waved her hand. A

swirling mist extended to the tea kettle. A phantom-like hand formed, grabbing the handle and filling the cup. Steam danced into the air as it floated straight to her. She took a long sip, relaxing on the chair.

"What's the plan?" I asked.

"I have two things to tell you," she replied and placed the cup down. "But first, tell me, did you arrange the ball?"

"For the most part, yeah." I nodded grimly. Betsy's silence really irked me more than it should have. "The Head of Events will make this as memorable as we need it to be."

"Great, that's good news. I often like starting with that," she said. "Please don't overreact, for what I'm about to tell you is only partially alarming."

I leaned forward. A dread colder than Hazel's presence struck me. "Partially alarming? What do you mean?"

"Numerous hairline fractures have been detected in the entirety of the hotel's premises—"

"WHAT?" I exclaimed, jumping to my feet. "The entire hotel? We need to get the people out! Is the hotel going to collapse? WE HAVE TO EVACUATE—"

Hazel calmly took the cup. "Would you threaten me with eviction if I slapped some sense into you? You're acting more hysterical than a family with a bewitched pressure cooker."

I blinked. Her response was nearly puzzling. "What? Bewitched pressure cooker?"

"The hotel isn't in immediate danger, Avira," Hazel explained as if her word choice made that obvious. "In reality, it is a good thing. The Illusion Shifter is looking for a window and is subtly extracting the building's essence."

I slowly sat back down. "Oh..."

"Yes, and a window is what we will give them." Hazel

lifted her hand and formed a fist. A magical hologram of the hotel bloomed before my eyes. It displayed each layer with frightening clarity. Words solidified, my eyes latching on the very top floor.

5th floor: Storage

"Storage?" I blurted out.

Hazel frowned slightly. "Yes? Did you not know that?"

I hesitated. "Um, yes."

The Restricted Area was a storage area? Why did that make so much sense? Of course, Uncle Julian would empty it before I arrived.

Hazel stood up, ignoring my response. I directed my attention to the remaining floors.

4th floor

3rd floor

2nd floor

1st floor

Cellar

"The ball will take place in Echo Ballroom," Hazel started. "All of the guests will be there as well as the necessary staff. Everyone else who does not have a job to do must leave. You can arrange that, right?"

"A paid leave for the rest of the day?" I rephrased. "I should be able to? I don't think my uncle has done such a thing before."

"He hasn't, nor do I think he would permit it, but he is not here," Hazel said matter-of-factly. "I don't know where the Illusion Shifter will anchor itself, so we need to know the hotel's sections are mostly empty. "

She extended her fist into an open palm. The sparkling hologram zoomed into Echo Ballroom. The rest of the hotel became a faint outline as several dots blinked to life. A large

S appeared at the front of the room and a large *C* appeared in the center. I assumed those were our positions.

"This is where you come in," Hazel began. "You seem rather confident in your tracking ability so listen to me carefully. You must be in the ballroom and track the Illusion Shifter at my signal."

I looked at the numerous dots. A sliver of tension looped around my muscles.

"In the ballroom," I repeated. "With all those people in there at once."

"Indeed," she affirmed. "You must be present as that is your role at these events. You should be able to lock onto the Illusion Shifter's exact movements."

Her eyes lingered on the owl statue. Something different distilled in her gaze.

"Right, I am very capable of that." My voice went higher than intended.

There would be roughly 450 individuals in the Echo Ballroom. Such a high volume of people… Simply spoken, but the execution was much harder. Tracking and Illusion Shifter in the presence of all of those guests would be short circuiting my ability. Overwhelmingly difficult. But I had to do it. Somehow and some way.

Hazel narrowed her eyes. "You don't sound convinced."

"I can do it, I was just…thinking," I said as reassuringly as possible. "Then what?"

"I will go find it." Hazel paused, her eyes meeting mine. "I suggest you follow me. I can't take my chances with any more tricks."

I retraced her words. "So we're trying to prevent the Illusion Shifter from anchoring?"

"That's correct," Hazel said, taking a long sip. "I'll try my best to intercept the connection. Once that's done, the Oldera Amulet will reveal itself."

"And what are you going to do with it?"

"Destroy it of course," she said icily. "Such things shouldn't be in anyone's hands."

I took in a subtle deep breath. "See you at 7 then?"

"Indeed you will." Hazel stood up slowly. "This case will be closed. That much I can assure you."

14

A Way or a Wall?

I slipped into Echo Ballroom long before the decorations were fully set up. For the first time, I did something Uncle Julian would never do. I refused to do my duties or take any complaints. The reasoning was simple. The present was in danger and I had things to do to stop it. One of which was finding a place to think. The vast room had a small stage at the very front. Enough to stand over the crowd and garner attention. I'd provide a proper description, but my attention to detail was far too scattered. I had too many things to do and I did not want to be seen.

Luckily, retreating to the stage was the best thing. There was a small, hidden section off to the right. A thick gold curtain expanded past the wall, providing a perfect nook to think. The several chandeliers glaring light nearly obliterated every shadow. I was grateful for the few that lingered behind the curtain.

The first thing I had to take care of was the remaining staff. It took an ungodly amount of time to compile a staff-wide alert. The amount of codes and verification walls Uncle

Julian set up was alarming. Even with the power of a Hotel Manager, demanding such an alert was nearly impossible. Thankfully for me, every code and puzzle was found in the manual. Unfortunately for me, time was relentlessly ticking.

I hardly had time to think about a proper excuse. A paid day off was enticing enough? I wouldn't question it if my boss decided to do something out of pocket for the proper dime. (Well, depending on the context, of course. Do not misinterpret.) However, I had to word it properly. Simply put, I wrote and sent:

Dear gracious staff members,

If you do not have a role in tonight's ball, please go home. The day will be paid and your duties will return to normal tomorrow.

With warm regards,

Miss Savio

I took in a shaky breath, my eyes stalled on the digital clock. 7 pm was fast approaching. I gingerly slipped the phone back into my pocket, forcing down any clouding emotions. The constant shuffling of busy feet thwarted the silence from enveloping me. A delicate scent of jasmine and sandalwood slowly permeated the air. The final preparations were falling into place. Hazel's plan was on the horizon. I imagine the guests lining the walls. A sinking feeling tugged at my senses. The plan was more dependent on my abilities than I was comfortable with. With Hazel, I tried to appear as if what she asked was possible. In theory, everything was. In execution? Natural flaws impeded certain outcomes.

If I wanted to pull off Hazel's plan, I needed to take a step back. Leaning against the wall, I closed my eyes. The continuous darkness soothed my sparking nerves. The clamorous sounds faded away from my attention. My mind's storm brought a new ship to the shore. A ship of mostly warm details, but among the sweetness was valuable knowledge. I needed to think about my childhood mentor, Arnoldo Davena.

The vampire general flashed across my memory with dizzying clarity. His scar-slashed face grew clear. He had gentle eyes for someone so rugged. A very faint smile always lingered on his gruff face. Threads of annoyance sewed between my desperation. I could only remember his dynamic lessons. Lessons in which I had to do something stuck with me. Yet, the solution to my problem wasn't something I personally executed.

A forgotten lecture was what I sought. My father spared no expense in hiring Arnoldo Davena. Since sensing was my only ability, sharpening my skill was crucial. But, younger me didn't understand why he hired a high-ranking war veteran. Rather than a sweet teacher from the nearby Condera Academy. I still didn't understand, but that was irrelevant for the moment. His lectures were fascinating but numerous. So much so the details had become muddled over the years. His droning voice was distant. I needed to find a way to reel his lessons closer.

My brows furrowed in concentration.

Pinpointing a single moving individual with a wall of people before me...

The exact term for it evaded me. Such a simple word impeded a quick internet search. Although, the internet would give me a vague description rather than a proper procedure. It sounded like a topic we covered. Before I went to Blixiton Boarding School. I forced myself to think about the study room.

A sharp memory flooded my mind. The unusual cozy embrace of the study room washed over my icy dread. Warmly lit by a dazzling star-shaped light fixture. The doodled wooden desk fizzled into reality. Tall burgundy walls erupted on either side of me. A multitude of books lined most of the walls. Few portraits were sparse, all depicting the generations of the Savio Family.

Mr. Davena stood before the tall, arched window. His hands were folded behind him as he looked out to the lavish green field.

"...It's not for everyone to attempt..." Mr. Davena's voice echoed. *"I used it in the War of Noxious. But be warned, you can completely detach the ability from your psyche."*

He turned to me, his gaze growing distant. *"Sifting through so many individuals. To sense past them. To extend my range and lock onto my target. An individual whose presence is strong enough to bypass a wall of people. This is why you need someone to latch onto. You need an ... "*

Realization washed over my mind.

Anchor. I need an anchor.

My eyes fluttered open. The solution to my problem was finally clear.

Hazel.

Hazel's puzzling presence was exactly what I needed. Never had I attempted such a feat. Mr. Davena was a skilled military general and I... I was the kid attempting to play detective in most eyes. But, as oddly as it seemed, I had found a chilling thrill to it. The ultimate test. One that meant more than simply proving myself.

"Miss Savio?" A masked staff member peered behind the curtain. "Preparations are ready. Here is a mic and your intro cards."

I glanced at his name tag. I didn't recognize Griffin in his masquerade attire. He handed me a crimson-red microphone and two simply decorated cards. I took it with a steady hand.

"Oh my, I forgot I had to talk," I muttered to myself. "Okay, then the ball continues without me?"

He hesitated slightly. "Not quite, Miss Savio. There are games to announce as well as other event preparations. First the greeting, and in 10 minutes I'll give you the following cue."

"Oh I see, thank you," I said with a stiff smile. "You'll shadow me for the night then?"

"Yes, I will give you your cards and necessary cues. I'll be near the stage at all times," Griffin said confidently.

"Thank you," I replied.

I eyed the ball's glittering name: Wise Masquerade Ball.

Without saying another word, he retreated. I took that as my cue to leave my hiding spot. A thorny nest of anticipation pressed against my chest. Each step I took felt like I was pushing through molasses. I gingerly placed the glittering mask on my face. My gaze was fixed on the muted brown stage. As soon as I entered the center stage, I was no longer greeted by the glaring light.

Slowly, I looked up. Awe rained over my cracking field of nerves. My eyes swept over the new grandeur. For a moment, I thought I was transported into an alternate world. Echo Ballroom no longer resembled the rough luxury I whisked past. The sharp brightness became a mystifying dim light. Chandeliers twinkled with a mischievous glint, almost winking. Scattered moonlight entered through the colorful stained glass. Balloons and vines wrapped the tall pillars, leading to the luminescent ceiling. The paintings… moved. The figures within danced to a tune only they could hear.

The center floor was shimmering with what seemed to be

a low-placed mist. Tables were off to the sides. Centerpieces were holograms of what seemed like different magical terrains. Different color skies and grounds. Shimmering and twinkling, it allured even the most impatient of eyes. Statues of various owls clad in armor towered above, nearly blending in with the pillars.

To the far left, musicians awaited their cue, ready to perform an equally enchanting piece. Echo Ballroom looked as close to perfection as it possibly could be. Awe continued to swirl with the impending doom that harbored my senses. I could almost see the people dancing. But with the start of the ball, the chase would begin.

"Doors open in two minutes!" a staff member called.

My shoulders stiffened as I poised my gaze to the twinkling, grand door. Anticipation tugged at my legs. I felt as if I was awaiting a bomb to go off. Willingly waiting for it to go off.

"Cue music!" one shouted.

Gingerly, I moved forward.

"Open doors now!"

A mystifying piece began. A delicate piano filled the grand room. Tentative notes flowed, causing my thoughts to halt. It dimmed and grew stronger. Each note lightly echoed down and off the walls. The progressing piece urged anyone deeper into Echo Ballroom. I watched as the doors fully opened with the tiniest sliver of hesitance.

My grip tightened around the microphone. In came the guests like a tidal wave. Everyone appeared as if the ball had been planned for months. Heels clacked under the sound of joining strings. Masks glimmered like distant stars under the warm light. Candles lit at their entrance. Was Hazel already among them? Sensing so soon would obliterate my composure.

I wanted to believe I'd spot her, even with a mask. Mostly because I *needed* to spot her. Without her presence, the first step of the plan couldn't be executed.

The spotlight clicked, and a bright light cascaded over me. The abrupt shift drew their gazes like a magnet. I put my hand behind my back, curling into a tight fist. My grip grew clammy around the microphone. A storm crackled within me, threatening to tear the roof off of my suppressed emotions. The moment of truth had dawned. The time for the chase commenced the moment the clock struck 7.

The enchanting piece dimmed as Griffin cued me.

I cleared my thoughts taking in a subtle deep breath.

"W-Welcome to Wise Masquerade Ball. I am your gracious host, Miss Savio. Tonight is a night of magic. Of mystic and intrigue," I said as clearly as I could. "Allow yourself to be carried by the veil of mystery. Strangers are to waltz, to keep their identities secret, and to uncover the true treasure of the night. Embrace the unknown. Tonight is a night to stand with the present."

Applause roared as I finished speaking. I could barely focus on what I was saying. My eyes scanned the crowd. Where was she? Time was of the essence even if the night was young. The enchanting music commenced, pulling the crowd to the center of the ball. Indistinguishable chatter was aloft. Laughter filled the gaps of silence.

I took a small step forward. The stage gave a perfect overview of the waltzing guests. Was Hazel the type to dance first? The thought alone was absurd. Logically, she would come to find me. According to her plan, I needed to wait for her cue. But, no matter how much my gaze ironed the crowd, the Witch Detective was nowhere to be seen. The grand doors gradually closed, sealing in the guests.

Staff moved in and out of the seamlessly hidden back doors. Desperation clawed at my chest. Doubt dared to seep into my thoughts. What if the Illusion Shifter contradicted Hazel's logic once again? What if the Illusion Shifter was already in the ballroom? What if—

I stopped my flood of questions. I couldn't allow myself to circle without action. But what would be my next move? If Hazel didn't arrive soon, the entire situation could flip on its head.

Unless she went ahead without me? No... she wouldn't. Unless...

Unless our plan had already crumbled. Perhaps it crumbled the moment we thought of it. But if that was the case, then what? My eyes nervously flickered to the large moon-shaped clock. I could nearly hear the merciless ticking above the crowd. Time would continue to move unbothered by any conflict.

My gaze traced the waltzing guests. Dread danced to the same enigmatic piece within me. I recalled the fractures that finely littered the 5th-floor walls. Such an evident sign was hidden by the dim light. Any imperfection was untraceable to the naked eye. I wanted to believe that was a good sign. No traces of the Illusion Shifter's magic. My beads were dull. No light filled the crimson spheres.

I fought the urge to pace around the stage. Showing such notable signs of stress was a fool's move. For all I knew, someone was observing my every move. My next cue was slowly dawning. All I could do was stare at the clock.

15

A Familiar Menace?

My eyes were glued to the closed door. I almost appeared like a statue on the stage. Clutching a microphone and cue card like my life depended on it. Had the circumstances been different, I would have enjoyed Echo Ballroom's atmosphere. It wasn't often I was in a room with waltzing masked strangers. Yet, little did the guests know the trouble bubbling beneath the elaborate facade.

As the clock struck the awaited time, I took a tiny step back. I brought the mic closer, bringing into view the card. For a moment, nothing happened. The lit candles danced to a different tune as the guests continued to waltz. My gaze subtly shifted to Griffin. He stood rigidly in the shadows. His statuesque stance blended with the stillness blossoming around him. Motionless, his dark eyes unblinking. Confusion pierced my enveloping dread.

"Griffin?" I said in a loud whisper.

He didn't answer. He didn't blink. He stood there as if... *entranced?* My thoughts crawled as I watched him. But entranced by what? I stole a glance at my beads. The deep crimson dangled, yet something caught my eye. Even under the dim light, the beads tended to have a faint shimmer. However, the beads looked almost… dull. As if… As if the charm no longer worked.

My stomach sank. My gaze whipped to the crowd, my ears latching onto the music. It was… looping. The piece abruptly began as soon as the final note rang across the grand room. Did the guests not notice? How long was the piece? Surely, it had been playing for as long as I stood? Someone must have noticed? Or… or were they incapable of noticing?

Panic nearly broke through my crumbling wall of serenity.

"Griffin!" I shouted.

The brash sound of my voice didn't jolt him or the crowd. One transfixed; The others dancing to their doom. My eyes whipped from Griffin to the ground. The mist was thicker than before. Enveloping the marble tile like a slow-moving tidal wave. A low rumble severed the music's false serenity. The stage shook as if a giant drew closer.

"Hello?" I said into the mic. "Stop dancing at once!"

My desperation-streaked voice rang through Echo Ballroom. Nobody reacted to my commanding plea. A dreadful conclusion flourished. The Illusion Shifter had started. But where? As my thoughts raced, the rumbling intensified. I desperately looked at the closed door. Hazel wasn't coming. The plan… I had to see through it. I could not just wait and see as the hotel crumbled before my eyes. Panic jousted my remaining composure.

I roughly threw the microphone. The blaring screech pierced through the music. I needed to act quickly. I needed to pinpoint the Illusion Shifter. Even without Hazel, I needed to succeed. Failure wasn't an option.

I took in a ragged breath as I neared the edge of the stage. The constant quaking made my concentration play a deadly tug of war. Mr. Davena's warning flashed across my mind.

"...It's not for everyone to attempt...I used it in the War of Noxious. But be warned, you can completely detach the ability from your psyche."

I must. It has to be done.

Without hesitating, I closed my eyes. The ground began to rumble. My senses ignited like a match to gasoline. The wall of people crashed through like a raging sea's tidal wave. Each person rained into me like arrows. A sharp pain jabbed at my temples. I could feel every movement like a swarm of mosquitoes. Everything overlapped. Every step. Every arm swing. Every twirl. The feeling pushed against me. Stabbing deeper into my psyche. Pain thorned every thought.

My ability was bending beyond capacity. My mind felt like a rubber band about to snap. The wall of people kept multiplying. The world within dared to spin. The ground violently shook.

I gritted my teeth, pushing through. My nails dug into my palms as my fists tightened. The pain amplified. I charged through the barrier. The crowd wasn't endless. There had to be a break. I had to see past them.

"Come on," I said through gritted teeth.

I recalled the Illusion Shifter's presence. The raging fire that scorched my senses was a ghostly sensation. A recent memory I needed to pull into the present. The Illusion Shifter was out there. I just... I just had to—

SNAP.

My senses split into two. An anchor attached to my feet. A blizzard exploded in front of me. I saw past. The clash of fire and ice raged, filling my mind with a nearly impenetrable steam.

The ice sprinted closer to me. The seething fire expanded…
beneath me.

My eyes snapped open.

The cellar!

The room spun. The ground quaked violently. My senses crackled from strain. The chandeliers shook turbulently, threatening to fall with every passing second. Large fractures crawled up the once pristine walls. The Illusion Shifter had more than just started. The Illusion Shifter was beginning to *drain.* My senses crackled with strain. I needed to get out of the ballroom immediately!

I jumped off the stage, the wind whistling past my ears. My feet crashed through the thick mist, slamming onto the cracking floor. I tried to move, but my feet clung to the marble tile. I jerked my feet up, nearly losing my balance.

"What?" I muttered shakily.

The thick mist impeded my vision. A sharp warmth spread over my shoes and sunk into my feet. Desperation clawed at my chest.

"Dammit!" I shouted. "I need to—"

SHATTER.

The stained glass exploded. Shards flew like sharp rain. My eyes whipped above me. An owl soared with great power, multiplying in size before my eyes. It dove toward me like a spear. My eyes locked on its glistening gold talons. Was it an illusion? No. It couldn't possibly be. An icy breeze charged toward me.

I realized too late. It snatched me into the air like a rag doll. A strangled scream escaped my mouth. The wind whistled past my ears. My feet kicked wildly. The owl was speeding toward the shut door. The doormen stood rigidly at either side.

The talon's grip gradually loosened. Before I could react, the doors blasted open. Hazel appeared through the smoke. Her wide eyes locked on me. The owl let go at the last second. My stomach lurched as I whistled through the air. She dove as I crashed onto the ground. I slammed into the wall, coming to an abrupt stop. Adrenaline masked the pain of the impact.

Hazel's head whipped between the ball and I. By the looks of it, she did intend on attending the ball. She was far overdressed for a cataclysmic event. However, the shimmering emerald gown was certainly her color.

"I couldn't get in. The Oldera Amulet—"

"The cellar!" I interrupted, scrambling to my feet. "We need to get there, *now.*"

"The cellar?" she echoed, her hand tightening around the glimmering staff.

I nodded quickly. My attention grew scattered. The destruction of the Echo Ballroom was worse. Hairline fractures became deeply grooved cracks. Debris rained from the ceiling, fueling the impending doom. The ground was jagged as if someone destroyed a delicately placed puzzle. The warm lights flickered wildly like a small flame combating a relentless wind. How much more could the building take before...before... before it was too late?

I looked at Hazel. Her racing thoughts visibly clicked.

"Every single door is locked by the Amulet's magic," she said almost inaudibly, our gazes locking. "I have to force my way through. That's our only way into the cellar."

"Then what?" I asked quickly.

"One shot," Hazel said firmly. "Failure is not an option, Avira."

That wasn't a plan. That was the desired outcome. Yet, with the hotel threatening to collapse on us, thoughts weren't easily connected. Hazel stepped away from me. My hands clenched into tight fists. How could I help? In regards to magic, there was nothing I could offer. Not a single counterspell or support. But, I would help. Somehow and someway, the Oldera Amulet had to be stopped.

Hazel's hands lit. Luminescent chains wrapped around her arms, binding her staff to her grip. She forcibly struck the quaking ground. A sparking ring drilled the ground, creating a wide enough entrance. For the first time, I got a glimpse of the terror that awaited us. Even with a mere floor dividing us, the air was crackling with an unbridled energy. I could... *feel it.* The way ancient magic flared. The distinct sensation only magic could conjure.

"I'll go first," Hazel said over the rumbling.

She hastily tore off the excess fabric, creating a sharp pattern. Without saying another word, she dove through. She landed, her hand signaling to follow. I jumped after her. I fought the urge to shut my eyes as I fell through the jagged hole.

My feet crashed against the broken ground. Hazel's staff was the only source of unwavering light. Her expression was caught in a tight scowl. My gaze shifted to the intricate magic before me. For a moment, I couldn't process what I saw. The Oldera Amulet's true form was hidden by a light that rivaled the moon itself. The vast room suddenly seemed smaller. Mystifying and alluring, tendrils attached to everything like a massive web. Various objects were disintegrating as the Amulet drew power from it.

The Amulet's magic behaved like smoke with a physical bond. Almost like various slithering snakes coiling around a foolish prey. I had never seen such magic before. How could a single Amulet hold so much power?

My eyes darted. I suddenly understood why the Restricted Area was empty. Uncle Julian had moved everything to the cellar. The one place he knew I'd avoid. I wasn't fond of the gloominess cellars radiated. I liked it much less with an ancient Amulet inside. A different type of darkness encroached from the corners. Yet as odd as it seemed, there were no obstacles between the Amulet and us. Just the cluttered array of my uncle's most prized possessions.

The building groaned like a ship fighting an angry sea. With every second that passed, the Amulet was growing stronger.

"To the Amulet!" Hazel shouted.

I jumped into action. Yet as I swerved between the clutter, a blur struck me. Pain spiked in my back instantly. I slammed through tables, a strong light flashing. The blow forced the air out of me as I skidded to the wall. My head whipped up. My eyes locked on... me? A daze threatened to overtake my thoughts. Was I hallucinating? Did the blow knock the sense out of me? No. Certainly what I saw was real. Real to the extent it could attack me. The festering shadow fully solidified before my eyes.

Realization struck me. The last Illusion Shifter decided to play a different card. The shadow had become a peculiar version of me. The differences made my skin crawl with a new anticipation. Completely identical, but she lacked my essence. Her amber-yellow eyes were dull and empty. Her hands weren't hands, but knife-sharp claws ready to tear me into shreds.

I scrambled to my feet. I was backing closer to the wall. Dread clawed at every rumble of the building.

"An embarrassment," Anti-Avira mumbled. "An embarrassment to your family!"

My hands curled into fists. How was I supposed to defeat myself? How was I–

She began to move toward me. Her slow steps sent ripples across the cracked cement. My eyes darted to Hazel. Her attention was scattered. Her icy gaze could have frozen over the entire ocean. A new storm overtook her expression. A rage filled with desperation and something else, something I couldn't name.

FLASH.

Shock waves of pure energy flung toward us. Hazel's staff lit in defense. A massive shield sprung to life, narrowly protecting me. Anti-Avira beamed with a new kind of power. Magical bullets shot mercilessly from the Amulet. Hazel's fingers interlocked in different patterns. The shimmering shield narrowly deflected every attack. She was forcing her way to the Oldera Amulet. One way or another, she had to stop it. *We* had to stop it. Hazel's words rang in my mind.

"One shot. Failure is not an option, Avira."

My jaw clenched, my eyes focusing on Anti-Avira. The Amulet was using the fullest extent of its growing power. Her beads were glowing with a menacing blue light. A twisted fanged smile slithered across her face. My fists clenched tighter, my nails digging into my palms.

"You're weak," Anti-Avira repeated. "Too weak to be a detective. Too prideful to admit you're in denial. You're an embarrassment of a Savio."

I didn't speak. I allowed her words to resonate. My scowl deepened. So many times... So many times outsiders had told me that. I, Avira Savio, would be the one to crush the family name. To stain the name with my antics. My forbidden career. My unorthodox way of doing things. Her words bit into my mind.

"A long line of leading figures. Of impressive vampires changing the industry. But you… You're nothing without your sensing ability. You… You should just stand down and let this hotel crumble. Prove to your family you're *nothing*."

Every feeling I withheld exploded to the surface. Only a coward would let that happen. The hotel's guests depended on me. I couldn't allow it. I needed to fight. Not for pride, not because I wanted to prove her wrong, but because it was my *duty*.

I charged as fast as I could. The ground beneath me displaced at the sheer force. Anti-Avira darted at the speed of light. My mind raced with my movements. Her hand swung with deadly accuracy. The wind whistled as her claws sliced through the air. I attacked back. With all of my strength, my arms swung wildly. Each attack connected, yet she was unfazed. If anything, she was growing quicker. Far too quick. Far too strong. I nearly tripped over my feet trying to dodge. My burst of adrenaline was running slow. My movements were growing dangerously sluggish. The cellar shook violently as the Amulet pulsed. The ancient magic crackled and thundered.

Did I have a particular weakness? Would such a thing transfer over? Other than vampiric threats, the answer evaded me. I wasn't evenly matched. As every second mercilessly ticked, my chances of winning were growing slimmer. Her quick hands sliced through the air. The speed was a consistent blur. Her claws were mere inches away from slicing through the uniform.

What do I do— What do I do—What do I do—What do I do—

Realization struck me like a whip. The beads? Was she powered by the beads? How could I get close without getting utterly obliterated? I needed to slow her down somehow. My eyes darted around me. I needed something. I needed to grab something. Hastily, I slid past her. My hand clasped around the first thing I could grab. The fluffy texture threw me off, but I flung it.

The blanket expanded, slapping her across the face. The sudden darkness made Anti-Avira collapse like a puppet. She didn't try to take the blanket off. I didn't question it. I swiped the beads and then crushed them in my grip.

My victory couldn't be savored. The Illusion Shifter was defeated, yet the Oldera Amulet still stood.

16

A Dissolving Truth?

The Oldera Amulet pulsed with great power. In my battle against Anti-Avira, Hazel had barely made any progress. Her shield was beginning to crumble like ice slowly cracking. The Amulet's blasts were getting more potent. The hairs on my arm stood. Even at the distance, every ripple made my soul tremble. I could no longer look at the Amulet directly. The light seared in my eyes at every glance.

"It's too late, Hazel," a distorted voice rumbled. "My time has come to make things right."

That voice...

Realization slapped me across the face. The vibrant nightmare seeped into reality. That voice... that voice belonged to the nameless foe. Fragments of the nightmare flashed across my mind. Although the true context of their animosity was unknown, I knew one thing for sure. The moment the Nameless Foe entered, everything was over.

"No!" Hazel shouted, strain plaguing her voice. "It has not!"

I tried to look past the light. Her enemy was threatening to break *through*. Panic exploded like a volcano. The Amulet's waves were becoming more volatile. Bits of the ceiling were beginning to crumble. Large chunks of the wall spilled onto the cracked ground. I watched immobile. Hazel pushed through. Her shield continued to crumble as the Amulet grew brighter. Even without a willed effort, the crackling sensation of magic was overbearing. I tried to move but I couldn't. Were we going to fail? What was Hazel going to do?

"You can't run for long Hazel," the distorted voice taunted. "I will set things in order!"

His voice boomed, sending a fierce shot wave. Hazel went flying. Her shield shattered. She skidded across the jagged ground like a pebble thrown by a giant. I dashed to her.

"Hazel, are—"

The words were taken from my mouth. The reality I knew was whisked away by a deep fog. Something formed within the shimmer. A strong wind blew the raining debris into currents. I stared at the fog. For a moment, I wasn't sure what I saw. Hazel suddenly grabbed my arm, but I couldn't look away. The fog formed a perfect, glimmering moving image. A montage?

A young girl with wavy caramel hair ran in an open field. A small white owl jumped and flew around her. Her small hand loosely gripped a staff far too big for her. Several people happily stood around her; their faces were blurred to me. Slowly, most faded into the background. All but one. He seemed to be the youngest in the background, yet older than her by a few years. I stole a glance at Hazel, my thoughts connecting slowly. A different expression was etched into her pretty face. It was nearly... terror. A deep seeded terror. Her wide eyes were unfocused as if her mind was torn between the past and the present.

The fog pulsed, giving way to another figment of Hazel's

past. The wind grew stronger, and more cracks etched across the ground and ceiling. She looked older, but younger than her present self. Her purple eyes were… warmer. There was still a twinkle; a glimmer of hope even. But hope for what? Her hands were occupied with several books. An overloaded broom floated behind her. Several signs and open doors surrounded her. The words became clearer. All were various detective agencies. As she turned to each one, every door slammed shut. She flinched at the first two, yet more closed. The warmth in her eyes slowly disappeared. Her clothes grew more and more ragged.

The images fell and formed into something else. She was holding a key. A wisp of a smile tugged at the corner of her lips. A small house-like building blossomed behind her. The sign above it proudly beamed: Mystic Eye Investigations. Yet, in a blink of an eye, the agency was engulfed by a blue flame. The key dropped from her hand as she ran. The darkness began to encroach around her. Several hands reached for her, but only one got closer. An owl ring glistened, narrowly missing her.

"Failure after failure…" The Nameless Foe relished. "Have you come to regret crossing me? Now is your chance to plead for mercy!"

BOOM.

The fog collapsed thunderously. The searing light disappeared into a brightening ring. A portal blossomed between. For the first time, I saw the Oldera Amulet in all of its nightmarish glory. The silver frame glistened as it expanded. The sheer power threatened to collapse the cellar. Hazel squeezed my arm, yanking my attention away. A deep panic settled in her eyes.

"Listen to me!" she shouted over the maelstrom. "Get the

guests out somehow! I can hold the building, but not for long!"

Hazel didn't let me speak. She sprung to her feet, her staff slamming into the ground. Dazzling gold pillars shot from the ground. Vine-like streams interwove the various cracks. That was it? I was supposed to run away? No, no, I couldn't. I had to do something more. Anti-Avira's words ricocheted in my mind. She had spoken painful truths. I was nothing without my sensing ability. Yet, was it denial? I was capable of more than that. Deep inside, my soul spoke for me. Spoke in a language only instincts would understand.

BOOM.

Another shock wave nearly swept me off my feet. A leather boot began to push through the portal. The boot glimmered menacingly as the tip struck through.

"No," I said.

Hopelessness clutched my chest. I felt something. I felt an urge to rush forward. To do something. Something within me was cracking. No way was the hotel about to collapse under my supervision. My hands grew searingly hot. Something bubbled vigorously within me.

I walked past Hazel.

"What are you doing?" she shouted. "You must—"

Her voice faded. My vision tunneled to the Oldera Amulet. I watched as time slowed. The foot was about to meet the ground. My instincts took over. I dashed toward it. _An intense wave of heat washed over my arms. A stabbing pain collected at my palms. My bones vibrated with a new sensation. I dove, clasping the Amulet with my hands. Something snapped within me. I screamed. A blinding white light flashed, searing my vision. Before I knew it, I could no longer feel the ground.

* * *

It would be a lie if I said I knew what happened. My consciousness slowly dripped back, yet I didn't open my eyes. A thick blanket smothered my thoughts. I couldn't think. I could just... *feel it.*   A diminishing wave of heat lingered on my arm. The ground had the slightest tremble as if still shaken from an intense force. A distant buzzing sound hovered over the scattered silence. All of the energy within me had been completely drained. Exhaustion that went far beyond me nestled. What did I do? My other senses slowly woke up. I had an incredibly metallic taste in my mouth. Similar to the ones humans attributed to blood, but in my case that was a delight. The taste was far more brittle. My mind crawled uphill to reality.

What happened?

Some of the energy slowly replenished, enough to move. My hand instantly met the floor. My mind slowly made sense of what happened. The last thing I could remember was a... blast. An intense heat that spiked in my palms. The way my hands curled around the activated silver Amulet. Then... then what? Did I get blasted into oblivion? Was I under the hotel's debris? Did I... fail?

I almost didn't want to open my eyes so soon. I wanted to wait a little longer. But what good would that do? I had a lingering pain in my arms and back. But other than that, I wanted to believe I was relatively unscathed. Gathering what was left of my courage, I slowly opened my eyes.

I blinked a few times, my vision clearing. Much to my surprise, my eyes met a black charred ceiling. The blast... The blast had happened. Yet, what I saw wasn't destruction. The ceiling was deeply cracked. The walls weren't threatening to collapse. All had a deep black soot as if some sort of explosive went off. The air crackled as if it housed electricity. The buzzing came from the overly bright light fixtures. The… The hotel was still standing?

Did we succeed? Where's Hazel?

As if my thoughts summoned her, she appeared beside me. Appeared? Perhaps she was there the entire time and I didn't notice.

"Good," Hazel said lightly. "I was starting to get worried."

I sat up abruptly. A heavy daze blanketed my thoughts. My head throbbed but to a bearable extent.

"D-Did it work?" I tripped over my words. "Are you alright? Is the hotel okay? Did—"

Hazel put a hand over my shoulder to stop me from getting up. "Relax, you'll hurt yourself. 7 Moons isn't in danger nor is the present. You… did it."

"I did?"

I looked at my hands. A burning sensation still peppered my skin. The tiniest cuts glowed in my palm before healing. Confusion berated my thoughts.

"I did what exactly?" I asked slowly.

Hazel didn't answer me immediately. A wisp of a smile tugged at the corner of her lips. For a moment, she seemed at a loss for words. Her gaze bounced between me and the charred ground. Pieces glittered even under the dim light. Was that the Oldera Amulet? Unmistakably, the silver glittered in jagged shards.

"An energy blast," Hazel said, her brows scrunching slightly. "Did you know you were capable of that?"

"Well, no. I never thought I'd have energy blasts in my itinerary," I said honestly.

"If it wasn't for that blast, this would be a very different story," she said, her gaze growing distant. Her attention fixed back to me. "I should thank you. If you hadn't insisted after the incident in room 322, things would be very different right now."

My brows raised in surprise. That was the first time anyone had ever thanked me for meddling. For a moment, I thought I misheard her. But for my own sake, I decided not to question it.

"Oh, uh, no problem," I responded. "It would be nice to put on a resume."

Hazel actually laughed for once. The sound was almost foreign. "Perhaps yes, but it would do you no good. Nobody knows about my cases besides myself."

"Trust me, it would do me no good either way,"

In the whole situation, I forgot about Cromwell and my forbidden career choice. It was nearly hard to believe a mere three days had gone by since I became a Hotel Manager. 4 days since I infiltrated Armeli's Black Market. Huh… Time really was an illusion. With so many things that had gone down, my hope for zero one-star reviews was nonexistent.

The third day concluded with a literal bang. I was sure the 7 Moons Hotel cellphone had been fried by the blast. I would have to get a new phone to see if I gained a new punishment. As clarity settled, my eyes fixed on the rest of the destruction. Shockingly, everything was intact for the most part. Even the things I saw disintegrated regained their original shape. The only thing that was broken were Uncle Julian's self-recorded songs. It had been years since I last saw it. (For which I'm sure I spared many ears.) Several scattered footsteps marched toward the cellars' now-released opening.

"The staff?" I said more to myself.

Hazel glanced at the door and walked to the sparkling shards. She smashed each one with her foot.

"You can never be too safe." She walked back and gave me a hand. "And Avira, don't worry about the staff. Just counter their questions with one of your own."

Easier said than done. A few odd things could be ignored, but it was a hotel-wide threat. A threat that we miraculously quelled. I nearly felt compelled to issue them some sort of explanation. Something that would put their mind at ease.

"I think you should go," I said with a smile.

"Right," Hazel agreed. "I'd like to speak to you tomorrow. There's a few matters to discuss."

I nodded.

There were more than a few things to discuss. More questions on my behalf. Many I had to sift through before deciding what was appropriate to ask. Without looking back, she slipped to a slightly indented wall. Subtly, she slipped the panel and walked into the inner walls. As soon as she left, the cellar's doors flung open. Betsy and Onyx barreled in along with several unfamiliar faces. They all held weapons and had an impeccable formation. Onyx's fierce expression crumbled to bewilderment.

"What happened?" Betsy blurted out, her eyes fixing on my disheveled appearance. "What happened to you? Are you okay?"

Any prior anger she held had completely dissolved. Before I could speak, her hands flung out into a tight hug. Pain spiked in my back. More due to slamming into the wall than Betsy's forceful embrace. She pulled away, her eyes darting to assess the damage.

"I'm fine," I said quickly. "The issue is completely taken care of."

"Clearly," Onyx said, turning to the armed people behind him. "You're dismissed."

Already? How strange. The armed people didn't hesitate to turn around. They didn't inquire at all. They just accepted my word and that was it? Were such incidents normal in 7 Moons Hotel to the point staff don't ask questions? Not even out of curiosity?

His expression darkened. None of his eyes could meet mine. He looked like he was about to explode. Betsy took a very small step away.

"What is it—"

"I'm so sorry, Miss Savio!" As soon as those words left his mouth, his rough hands sprung toward me, tightly clasping my own as he collapsed to his knees. "Fire me! I'm incompetent! I'm the worst Head of Security the world has ever seen!"

Tears sprung from his many eyes. I wanted to speak but he wouldn't let me.

"You warned me! You told me there was something wrong and I didn't believe you! I—I—I really didn't see anything! Anything at all! Nothing came through the cameras. My crew didn't see anything out of the ordinary. Everything was normal! I swear on my life!" He squeezed my hands tighter.

Now it was my turn to be bewildered. I looked at Betsy for guidance, but she too looked like she wanted to apologize. It truly wasn't necessary. They did nothing wrong.

"Onyx," I said as gently as I could. "I'm not firing you. It was magic beyond our knowledge and capacities."

His eyes widened. "You're not firing me?"

I shook my head. "It was—"

"Oh you don't have to explain," Betsy interrupted. "Mr. Savio never gives us accounts of special incidents, you don't have to either."

"No, really. I feel like I should give you an explanation. Everyone was at risk, that's the least I can do." I pressed on.

Onyx slowly rose to his feet, releasing my hands. He stood stiffly beside Betsy. They both looked more confused than I expected.

"Miss Savio," Betsy said. "You saving 7 Moons is enough for us to know everything is fine now. I… I should have known something was going on. I just… I thought you were trying to make things more interesting for the guests."

A daring question traveled to my mouth. "These incidents… are normal?"

Onyx and Betsy exchanged a glance. "Mr. Savio just solicits our help under Code 996. No questions asked, but we perform what is required of us."

"I see.." I held my tongue. "I'm sure Mr. Savio will be here soon after how things panned out."

There was a network. A network I barely understood. And from the looks of it, I probably wouldn't get a chance to.

"And the hotel is okay?" I asked slowly. "The guests aren't planning on making a collective lawsuit?"

"The hotel is completely fine! Besides the random hole in the hall and the shattered glass," Betsy said. "The guests are completely fine, just incredibly hungry."

My eyes widened. "What? Really?"

"Yes, Miss Savio!" Betsy gave me a warm smile. "Thank you for your hard work. You did great."

My eyes started to burn, but I withheld. "That's so good to hear."

"Oh and, don't worry about the rest of the ball. I have that taken care of." She reached for my hand and gave it a light squeeze. "Just go and rest."

"Rest," I echoed. "I'll… I'll go do that."

The walk from the cellar to the 4th floor had mundanely greeted me. Much to my relief, any damage the Oldera Amulet had done was entirely reversed. All I found was displaced dust and tilted paintings. Any minor damages were overlooked by my exhausted eyes. All the energy I had left was quickly draining from my being. Perhaps it was the shocking win that supplied me with enough energy to speak to Betsy and Onyx. My mind still buzzed with our victory. I was processing the situation at a snail's pace. We… succeeded. We actually defeated the Oldera Amulet. I could hardly believe it. The "how" was more puzzling.

An energy blast? It wasn't a rare vampiric ability by any means but for a Savio? I had somehow won the gene pool lottery. No matter how much I tried, I couldn't recall the last Savio who had that ability. My mother had super strength, which I inherited. My father's side, the Ordin Family, had Shadow Camouflage, which I did not have. But Energy Blasts? I couldn't wrap my mind around it. However, my body understood very well.

My limbs were like cinder blocks. My feet dragged across the carpet. I fought my eyelids. Each time I blinked I risked falling asleep. I could hardly stand straight. Every step required a hand against the wall. Alterin Hall felt endless.

I pushed through my exhaustion, finally reaching my room. As soon as my bed was within reach, I plopped onto it. A deep sigh escaped my lips. The moment I shut my eyes, a comfortable darkness embraced me.

17

A Moon's Phase?

Sleep had effectively restored my energy. So much so, that it appeared I had become a sleep-walker during the night. The last thing I remembered was falling on my bed. Yet as my eyes scanned the room, it became more evident that I did *more* than sleep. My body partook in a chaotic picnic. Several empty blood bottles decorated the sofa and floor. I had torn open a few cookie bunches. Only leaving behind a fine trail of crumbs on the nightstand. The TV was on, blasting the forsaken informational channel.

With the lingering confusion dissolving, clarity brought the answer. It was the after-effects. The after-effects of unlocking a new ability in high-stress situations. Unlocking such abilities required a certain after-care. Usually, a family member or close friend would help. The process was simple but incredibly necessary. I had completely forgotten about it.

The caretaker would brew a special tea, make sure they ate enough, and finally, make sure the person fell asleep in a certain position. I did none of those things. Nor did I think to ask. Going to bed with hunger awoke my body for a midnight snack.

I wasn't necessarily upset with that. I felt… *great*. Any ache or bruise became a distant sensation. A cool breeze brought a fleeting serenity to the messy room. I was relaxed, but that too would be fleeting.

The gentle sun indicated a still-settling morning. That meant I had time for two important things. Breakfast and a proper evaluation of what happened last night. As I rose to my feet and proceeded to freshen up, I allowed my thoughts to flow freely.

For a moment, I wasn't sure where to begin. Perhaps it was because I couldn't wrap my mind around a simple fact. We… won. Barely, but the victory was ours. Much like my previous wins, I couldn't entirely savor it. There were still many things floating inconclusively.

My mind was pulled to the fog I witnessed. The Oldera Amulet had done more than wreak havoc. It had given me a window into Hazel's past. A past I doubted I would have discovered so soon. Or ever, for that matter. The abrupt insight left me with more questions than before. I had to be cautious of what I asked. Yet, the more I thought about it, a new question surfaced.

Was it even my position to ask?

I slowly connected the underlying dots. Things I didn't give much mind to suddenly made sense. Hazel Caine was a Witch Detective who struggled to find an agency. So much so, that she established her own. Only for it to get engulfed by flames. All of her hard work vanished quicker than expected. My mind flashed back to her ragged clothes. Did… Did that mean she didn't have a place to stay? To work?

Were those questions within our amicable boundaries? The night she arrived, Hazel got a free stay due to accumulated points. How did the amount of stays coincide with Mystic Eye Investigations? Had each stay truly been for a case? Or was it simply to… well, stay?

The rest I saw within the fog, I wouldn't inquire about. However, denying my simmering curiosity would be a disservice to me. I was curious. Immensely curious. Who chased after her? Who was the boy in the background? Who was the Nameless Foe? I had only seen his boot, but I found myself pulling away from the thought. It felt counterproductive to give him my attention. The Oldera Amulet Case was solved. His name was no longer important. Yet, the damage he did still lingered. Was he also behind the fire? If so, why? What was the conflict between them?

The terror in Hazel's eyes had spoken a thousand undecipherable words. I only knew the Witch Detective for mere days. That was hardly enough time for someone to willingly spill their past. Yet, as oddly as it seemed, I found my curiosity quickly dissolving.

I didn't need to know. Hazel didn't owe me a single explanation. It was none of my business. As I put on the silky blazer, another thought dared to push through the clutter. If it was true. If Hazel truly didn't have a place to stay…

No. I was getting ahead of myself. The 4th day officially started. Guests had already started to check out as I got ready. That meant… all of my one-star reviews were waiting for me. I was nearly grateful the blast obliterated the 7 Moons cellphone. A bitter taste raided my mouth. Cromwell's smug expression flashed across my mind. My efforts did not count for him. They never would. But to me, they certainly did. He would never know what happened in 7 Moons Hotel. But I would. Whatever foolish punishment he had, I face it. Demolish it even. I promised myself that.

I adjusted my sleeves in the water mirror. My face was no longer ghastly. I took in a deep breath and practiced my smile once more. The last walk from my room to Savio Office as Hotel Manager. The least I could do was look cheerful. Given the previous circumstances, I had every reason to be. Without looking back, I stepped out.

The hall was much more active than in previous days. Staff walked up and down. Many smiled as I made my way to the elevator. I was glad to see everyone in such high spirits. It was almost hard to believe mere hours ago some had been under an ancient spell. I wondered how aware they were of everything. Or how they acted when the spell was broken. Were they disoriented? Or did they not notice? Perhaps a blend of both?

The elevator dinged at my arrival. To my surprise, I found a beaming Griffin. He looked much better than when I last saw him. Griffin stood straight, but his shoulders were relaxed. Any lingering effects of the spell weren't visible on the surface. If anything, he looked as if he had the best night's rest.

"Miss Savio! Lucky me running into you!" he exclaimed cheerfully. "I didn't expect to see you so soon! How are you feeling?"

I hesitated, my brows raising in a subtle surprise. How much of last night did he know about? Surely, I didn't tell Onyx or Betsy about unlocking an ability. I must have looked quite terrible for them to assume I needed the entire morning.

"I'm doing good," I said stiffly, stepping in. "Nothing of importance."

"Betsy told me you had a massive headache, which is why I didn't see you for the rest of the night," Griffin clarified. "I was actually coming to slip you a note."

Relief quickly dissolved as my eyes flickered to his hand. Pinched between his fingers was a lightly folded note. The crisp white paper nearly beamed against the black of his gloves. I took the note from him slowly.

"It's just a reminder to go to Savio office immediately, but looks to me like you're doing that already," he explained.

I quickly unfolded the paper and read:

Dear Miss Savio,

I hope you have been freed from your headache. Please go to Savio Office as soon as you're able to. There's an important notification awaiting your attention. Please review it before proceeding with anything else.

With Warmest Regards,

Sub-Management

My stomach sank deeper than my teeth on the bottles last night. I managed to smile at Griffin who awaited a response.

"Thank you, I'll see to it immediately."

"Ah, I'm sure it's nothing of real importance," he said reassuringly. He probably noticed how my expression darkened as I read. "Sub Management is always cryptic. I think that's why Mr. Savio likes them so much."

"Can't deny that," I said with a stiff smile.

Griffin laughed as if he were reminiscing. He patted my shoulder. "Elusive group of people. You'll like them when you meet them."

"I'd like to agree with you," I said as the doors finally opened.

I gave Griffin a polite nod and walked out. He didn't know the real reason behind my sudden role as Hotel Manager. Thanks to Uncle Julian, none of them knew. Yet, that didn't shield me from the conclusion awaiting me. The note alone was a confirmation. My time as Hotel Manager had come to an end. Thinking otherwise would be delusional of me. I hardly knew what I was doing on Day 1. With the sudden magical conflict, my role as Hotel Manager took an abrupt back seat. Sure, I used my power to arrange things for Hazel. But did I work? There was a pile of papers I left unattended. I hardly knew any of the guests' names. The few complaints I addressed were far too minimal to gain some sort of positive reputation. I hardly spoke to anyone. I simply… smiled.

Did I expect such an outcome? Deep inside, I did. Just… Not so soon. At least within the month. Of course, I didn't want to give Cromwell that pleasure. But given my recent luck, I would have racked up a one-star review per week. How did Uncle Julian do it? Perhaps I should have paid more attention all those summers ago. Although, I doubt he dealt with many magical crimes. Perhaps he dealt with more grounded conflicts. Something along the lines of paintings arguing with guests. Or toilets exploding?

A deep sigh escaped my lips as I neared Savio Office. My pace was a snail's crawl to the door. I didn't expect to have such hesitance so tightly wrapped around my legs. Just earlier, I was determined to face Cromwell's punishment. Somehow, that courage was beginning to waver.

Stop it. You're giving Cromwell the satisfaction.

I shook my head, shaking away the icy sensation. As soon as I walked in, my eyes locked on the new phone and the awaiting computer. Taking in a subtle deep breath, I snatched the phone. The screen lit at my abrupt touch. In dazzling red letters, the 7 Moons Review Monitor pulsed the notification. I turned my back to the open door and stole a glance at the calendar. I kept my promise. Even with the odds against us, I still returned to the office. To my satisfaction, I decided to place a heavy *x* on the fourth day. Tossing the pen aside, I directed my attention back to the phone.

Without hesitating any longer, I clicked the notification. The screen flooded with a rich burgundy. A stark yellow loading bar teased me as it slowly reached completion.

"Ah dammit," I said, turning the screen away from me.

It felt like tearing a band-aid off a still-healing wound. My courage to look at the small screen was draining quickly. The truth was a glance away. All I had to do was see the one-star reviews. But then what? Would Francis come get me? Would *Cromwell* come? Oh dear, I could just imagine the look on my mother's face. Then what? If I told her the situation, she would understand? What would my father think? What—

A sudden knock at the door made me jolt. "Miss Savio?"

I turned around to see Betsy. She had a warm smile on her face and a gift basket wrapped in her hands.

"How are you feeling?" she asked, lingering by the door.

"Much better," I strained a smile. "Thank you for last night."

"Eh, it's nothing. I pride myself in magical balls!" Betsy said happily. "I'll get going. Much to do, little time to do it."

She went to turn away but an idea snatched my thoughts.

"No wait!" I called after her. Having someone else pull the band-aid off was the best thing I could think of. "Do you have a moment?"

"Certainly." Betsy placed the basket on the desk. "What do you need?"

I handed her the phone and took a seat. "Just tell me how many one-star reviews are on there."

Confusion flashed across her face, but she complied with my request. The burgundy light reflected off of her white shirt. I could see hints of yellow, belonging to the stars I surely didn't receive. Anticipation bubbled as I watched her eyes move. A slight frown scrunched her brows.

"One star?" she repeated.

"Yes." I clasped my hands together. "How many?"

"Um…"

"Betsy, please tell me." I grabbed onto the armrests tightly. "I feel like I'm about to combust."

"There's…" Betsy smiled slightly. "None."

I blinked at her. "I'm sorry, what?"

"None," she repeated, handing the phone back to me. "Many five and fours stars. A few three stars and only one two stars."

"Oh," I croaked.

"Is that all?" Betsy asked, still smiling.

I nodded. She left, gently shutting the door. My eyes were wide as I stared at the screen. Betsy wasn't lying, yet I couldn't believe my eyes. Was I hallucinating? No, two people couldn't hallucinate the same thing at the same time.

"There's none?" I muttered in disbelief.

My eyes relatively traced the signifying zero.

Zero.

Z e r o.

Unbridled relief exploded. I shot to my feet like a firecracker.

"YES!" I shouted. "TAKE THAT CROMWELL!"

I punched the air. I jumped. Oh, victory was so, so, so sweet. Nothing could ruin it. Not a single one-star review. Even with a magical enemy, not a single guest felt compelled to give me their lowest rating. I was tempted to question it but didn't. My eyes were burning with such relief. Two wins in a row? And a win I could actually enjoy? Was I dreaming? No, no I wasn't.

That meant… If I dared… I could ask Hazel. I could still help her. I could even… I could even be her… assistant? I had a knack for it, didn't I? Cromwell's cases and Hazel's wouldn't overlap. Cromwell nor his agency took on a magical case. As odd as it was for an Elvin man, he wanted nothing to do with it. That gave me a massive space. A space to do what I had always thoroughly enjoyed.

The Anonymous Helper would make a victorious comeback. However, I was getting ahead of myself. Such a thing would only come to fruition if, and only if, Hazel agreed. If she was truly in need of a place to stay. If what I saw was true… she wouldn't turn me down, would she?

I glanced at the clock above the stained glass. Colorful lights were scattered across the face. The morning had fully settled. Would it be best if I waited for the meeting request? Or was it better if I made one myself? My proposition would be better made on the 5th floor. I wanted to believe the vast emptiness would aid my argument. I had no intention of refilling the Restricted Area with Uncle Julian's clutter. Nor did I have the intention of going back into the cellar. I truly couldn't think of a better use for the 5th floor.

Mystic Eye Investigations. Reborn within the walls of 7 Moons Hotel.

The mere thought gave me chills.

"Alright," I said to myself. "I'll send the note first."

Quickly I scribbled down the simple request.

Hazel,

5th Floor. Noon.

Sincerely,

Avira

I folded it and walked to the door. I waved down Griffin. "Would you bring this to room 322?"

"Will do, Miss Savio," Griffin said, quickly retreating.

With that done, I only had to wait. I glanced at the pile of paperwork. If I truly wanted to make everything work, I would have to become the best Hotel Manager I could possibly be. My updated schedule for the day was blinking on the computer. It was the same task as the other two days. For once I welcomed the routine.

18

A New Chance?

I arrived at the Restricted Area a few minutes earlier than intended. Perhaps because I found myself walking faster than usual. I was quietly pacing on the vast floor. My mind circled my approach. How would I start the conversation? Hazel mentioned she had a few things to discuss with me. If she started first… It would give me some more clarity, wouldn't it? What if I misinterpreted everything? What if I was getting ahead of myself? I halted my thoughts and eased to a stop.

I took a long look at the 5th floor. Within more calm circumstances, I noticed how different it looked from other floors. It almost reminded me of a forgotten ballroom. Wall-less, but not in an off-putting way. The grandeur from the lower levers had only increased. Scattered colorful light traveled from the circular windows on the ceiling. The towering walls shimmered with a subtle elegance. The paintings on the ceiling looked more alive than before. If I tried hard enough, I could see them move in sync with my motions.

If the paintings were sentient, I wondered what stories they would tell me. Surely, something interesting was—

The panel clicked as it swung open. Hazel slowly entered, her feet making a faint clack on the floor. I managed a genuine smile. Although she didn't smile, she didn't scowl either. If anything, her steps were tentative. Almost as if she was hesitant about something. Without having to think hard, I understood why. I had seen something she wouldn't have shared. I wasn't a stranger to the feeling. I too had a blanket of hesitation over my intentions.

"What an interesting spot," Hazel remarked. "I thought you'd prefer the comforts of your office than this place."

"I thought it would be better to talk here," I said, walking to her. "I think I'd get interrupted constantly down there."

"I don't doubt it." Hazel nodded slowly. "Alright, let's start, shall we? I am not one for small talk."

Hazel had her staff tucked behind her. With a swift moment, a chair appeared behind me. A coffee table clicked between us. A random teapot dropped out of thin air, clinking on the wood. She sat down nonchalantly. Although her demeanor was mostly neutral, her brows were slightly scrunched.

"There's something I wanted to ask you," Hazel started slowly. She reached for the porcelain cup. "Before we met at the ball, I saw an owl."

"You didn't do that?" I asked.

She shook her head slightly. "I didn't get a proper view. I really just saw you flying through the air."

My mind flashed back to the images in the fog. The shimmering feathers burned into my memory. My hands slowly clasped together. I knew very little about witch customs, but a thought formed.

"Hm," I muttered. "Do you have a familiar?"

Her brows scrunched subtly. Her gaze shifted to the shimmering pink tea. She observed it as if her thoughts were hidden within the glittering liquid.

"Had," she said wistfully. "I haven't seen him in so long. When I saw the owl, I just… thought. Odd, I never am hopeful about such things, but… did you get a good look at it?"

I paused for a moment. It truly looked like a blur in the chaos. I could still feel the ghostly grip of the talons on my shoulders. I was so bewildered, the memory was extra crisp in my mind.

"A pearly white owl," I said slowly. "Very sharp gold talons."

"Gold?" The hope pulled away from her eyes. "Oh, I see."

Hazel gently placed the cup back down. Although I wasn't sensing her, a new type of chill settled on the 5th floor. It seemed like the past had more than just presented itself through the fog. It made a point to poke at Hazel in several painful ways. Her gaze fixed past me. Her lips twitched as if she wanted to say something else.

"Whatever that was, then I'm glad," she said, although she didn't sound like she meant it. "Besides that, I wanted to thank you."

"Oh, you don't have to. Anyone would have done what I did," I responded.

"No, they wouldn't. I didn't expect you to take such a risk," Hazel said more to herself. "Did you know it would work? Have you always had energy blasts? Or about the possibility of you unlocking that?"

I shook my head. "No. What happened there was a massive whim. I was either going to break the Amulet or get a foot in my face."

Hazel didn't laugh. She nodded as if she figured as much. "There's something I need to speak to you about."

I leaned forward. Would the conversation finally give me

an opening? I just needed a moment. A small moment and I would ask.

"What you saw…" Hazel started, her tone shifted. "What you saw was not meant for your eyes."

Her voice was speckled with finality. I swallowed down my brewing nerves and nodded at the Witch Detective. My hopes for a natural segue quickly dissolved. As much as I didn't want to pry, I still had to give my proposition. I stiffly sat back on the chair.

"I see," I said rather rigidly.

"I would have never willingly divulged my past so soon," she continued, her words resonating with sincerity. "Some things don't need to be known at all."

I hesitated. Hazel was making it clear. Our teamwork had ceased last night. I was no longer welcome to meddle in her business. Yet, her blunt delivery was a vague confirmation. What I had seen was true, but to what extent? The words circled my mouth, yet my voice came out much more uncertain than I expected.

"So, is it, um, true?" I asked gingerly. "That—"

"That I'll be checking out later today? Yes, now that the case is over, there's no reason for me to be here any longer."

My eyes widened. "But you booked—"

"I know," Hazel said flatly, rising to her feet. The chair behind her disappeared in a gentle shimmer. "But I don't dwell in one place longer than I need to."

I rose to my feet. "But—"

"Avira, thank you for what you did," Hazel's voice softened. "I really am grateful. 7 Moons Hotel is finely protected under your care. I dare say even more so than with Mr. Savio."

She gave me a friendly nod and turned around. The words I

didn't have a chance to say vigorously bubbled within me. The conversation ended too soon. I didn't have a chance to ask. To at least know more. But no, I couldn't let her leave.

"Stay," I said abruptly, my voice echoing.

Hazel turned around. Her expression cracked with genuine confusion. "What?"

"Y-you don't have a place to stay, don't you?" I asked quickly. "Then stay… here."

"I'm not following," she said slowly. "What you saw is not a burden for you to uphold. I am fine on my own."

I took a step closer. "So you have a place to stay? To work?"

Hazel hesitated, her eyes diverting away. "I have… places. But Avira, like I said before, there are some things you don't need to know."

"It wasn't right," I said firmly. "It really sucks that all your hard work ended up in flames. That not a single agency wanted your help. I know I just met you, but I'm sure you're an even better Witch Detective than those idiots."

A new emotion distilled into her purple eyes. She blinked as if I spoke nonsense.

"What you saw… It's…" Her voice was almost a whisper.

"You can stay here," I repeated, this time with more confidence. "You can set up Mystic Eye Investigations in the Restricted Area. We can figure out how to get clients up here. You can stay in the room you are now, at least until you get back on your feet."

I was thinking of something more convincing to say when I heard a sudden fluttering above me. My gaze locked on the shimmering white owl. He nearly blended into the framework. Hazel's eyes fixed on the owl. Her thoughts nearly distilled into the surface of her gaze. Indecipherable to me, but clear to the owl. He swooped down from the high perch and landed between us.

"I would listen to Miss Savio, my dear Hazel," the familiar's voice was deep. "It isn't often you stumble upon a kind-hearted individual."

"A-Astor?" Hazel's voice cracked. She took a small step forward. She stared at him intently. Her stony expression crumbled to something I couldn't name.

Astor's light purple eyes looked like a distant galaxy.

"The one and only," he replied softly.

"So, so it was you," her voice shook. "You—you—"

"I sensed you were in trouble and decided I've waited long enough," Astor explained. "I would have arrived sooner but I couldn't get into 7 Moons. I had no choice but to break my way in."

He turned to me, giving me an apologetic look. Now that I saw him clearer, his talons were silver.

"It's completely fine. I've never been so grateful to see glass shatter," I said, my eyes lingered on his talons.

"Oh that," Astor chuckled slightly. "Nifty little spell. I wasn't going to harm you, especially after all you did to help solve the case."

"You knew?" Hazel asked in a daze. "You knew I was…"

"Of course I did, but I couldn't help you at the time. You weren't in any immediate danger," Astor said, his large eyes narrowing. "You have a habit of not accepting help."

Hazel's hands clenched the excess fabric of her pink dress. She looked like she wanted to protest but withheld. The tension in her eyes crumbled.

"I'm sorry," she said quietly. "For last time. Had I known I would have…"

"It wasn't your fault Hazel," Astor replied softly. "That's not enough to keep me away from the Caine family. It is my duty to help you from close by, and from the far, Ja—"

"Thank you," she interrupted, her voice had a hard edge to it. Then softly she said, "Really, thank you. It was nice… seeing you."

"I do not plan on leaving yet," Astor said. "Not until everything is effectively sorted out."

His large eyes flickered to me. So subtle, had I not been staring, I wouldn't have noticed.

A stiff silence fell between them. For a moment, hesitance cracked further her expression. It was almost like she didn't know what to do with herself. It was evident she missed her familiar. However, for whatever reason, she couldn't express it. Perhaps it was because I was in the room?

"Oh, I'm intruding, I'll be—"

"No, no," Astor replied. "I will take my leave for now and will return in the evening."

Before anyone could say anything else, he flew into the air and disappeared in a gentle purple shimmer. I cleared my throat. I didn't want to fall into an extended silence. Slowly, I folded my hands behind me.

"So, what do you say?" I prompted gently. "It's not a permanent thing, just for as long as you need it. While I'm here, the 5th floor is yours."

Hazel's eyes slowly moved away from the shimmer to the vast room behind me. She removed her hands from her dress.

"It's a good idea," she said with a small smile. "It's much better than floating above places."

"Really?" I nearly beamed but I managed to control the sudden high pitch of my voice. "Wait, *floating*?"

"It's a great location, but..." Her eyes fixed on me. "I'm assuming there's a catch?"

I broke into a smile. "Yes. Let me join in some cases. You don't have to pay me. I don't need the money."

"And if I disagree, you'll take back your offer?"

I shook my head. "Of course not, but you might find me very annoying."

Hazel let out a little sigh, but she didn't seem completely annoyed by the notion. Anticipation crackled as I watched her decide.

"Only select cases," she responded. "And in those cases, you must address me formally. I'd like to appear professional."

"You're really agreeing?" I nearly exclaimed. I couldn't believe my ears.

She extended her hand. "Deal?"

I took her hand in both of mine. "Deal."

19

Moonlight's Shimmer.

The night's concealing shadows fell over 7 Moons Hotel. The day had progressed with a new type of smoothness. Yet, even with the long hours and sporadic complaints, a smile didn't leave my face. My cheeks hurt, but I found the strain gratifying. For the first time since I arrived, I stepped out of 7 Moons' vintage walls.

The gently lit road looked endless from where I stood. The statues twinkled in the distance. The back of the sign buzzed faintly as distant cars made their way down the road. I faced the hotel, my shoulders completely relaxed. The crisp breeze brought a chill down my spine. Winter subtly settled within the pleasant nightfall.

I wasn't standing outside simply to stand. I was waiting for a particular moment. Each false moon twinkled on each pillar. But the full moon would settle on the 7th pillar as the clock struck midnight. Without the stress of the day, 7 Moons Hotel was truly a work of art. A single faint light lit in the Restricted Area. I glanced at the watch as the minute neared. As the moon crept to the pillar, Astor soared out of the 5th floor. I could faintly see a bundle of cards in his talons.

One fell out, dancing in the wind as it found its unknown location. An odd sense of pride surged within me.

I, Avira Savio, would be more of a detective than a delinquent. Case by case, I would prove that. Just you wait.

Acknowledgments

Woohoo! You made it to the end of the book! Thank you so much! I hope you enjoyed your stay at 7 Moons Hotel. Would you believe me if I said this story came to me because I bit my lip? I suddenly had the urge to write a story about vampires, and naturally, witches too! As you may have guessed, there are many more cases for Avira and Hazel to tackle! This one didn't have much investigating, but that's only because Avira stumbled upon Hazel's case. You can expect a proper case in the next book. Speaking of witch (pun intended), the next book will come out in October 2025!

I have many people to thank. First, thank you Mamá for helping me and listening to me drone on for hours about random WIP ideas. You're the best mom in the world.

Also, special thanks to Holly Dunn for creating the cover of my dreams! I haven't been able to stop staring lol! Thank you to Marc MacDonald and Lillian Sue for naming the agency and slogan respectively. I really wouldn't have been able to think of something better! Also, thank you to Kristin Wolf for helping me with the blurb! (Check her books out if you love great Regency romance novels.) Special thank you to Jessie Cunniffe for creating the Book Blurb Report Card! It really elevated the blurb.

And lastly, but certainly not least, thank you for picking up my lil indie novella. Thank you for reading indie books and supporting indie authors. I sincerely mean it.

About the Author

Laura Espinal Corpeno is a fantasy author who loves to write about determined main characters in magical dilemmas. Adding a twinge of humor, a pinch of mystery, and plenty of magic, Laura loves crafting stories for readers to escape. Since she was a child she knew she wanted to become an author. Her love for reading started with action-adventure books and since then, she has never looked back. When she's not writing, she's watching anime, trying to learn new languages, or embarking on random side quests.

Follow Laura on her writing journey as she transports the reader into unforgettable worlds with unforgettable characters.

You can connect with me on:

🌐 https://www.authorlauraespinalcorpeno.net

www.ingramcontent.com/pod-product-compliance
Lightning Source LLC
Chambersburg PA
CBHW032308310726
48973CB00008B/2565